The Girl in the Nile

A Mamur Zapt Mystery

Michael Pearce

Poisoned Pen Press

Poisoned Pen Press
6962 E. First Ave. Ste. 103
Scottsdale, AZ 85251
www.poisonedpenpress.com
info@poisonedpenpress.com

Printed in the United States of America

Chapter 1

"But," said Owen, "where is the body?"

"Ah yes," said the watchman, rubbing one horny foot up and down his shin.

"Ah yes," said the corporal, shuffling uneasily.

Owen waited.

"Well," said the corporal at last, looking out over the river to where a low mud shoal raised its back above the water, gray and wrinkled like a hippopotamus, "it *was* there."

"Well," said Owen, "it's not there now."

It had been a long, hot, fruitless morning. And now this! He boiled over.

"If this is some joke—"

The watchman looked as if he was about to burst into tears.

"But, effendi, it *was there*; I saw it."

"Or thought you did."

"Foolish man!" said the corporal, swiftly switching sides. "It was all a dream."

He gave the watchman a push. The watchman pushed him back.

"It was no dream!" he insisted. "I saw it with my own two eyes. A woman, on the sandbank."

"A woman!" said the corporal. "There, what did I tell you! It is time you got another wife, Abu. Then you would stop having these foolish dreams."

"I saw it plainly. On the sandbank."

"You saw something plainly," said Owen.

"It was a woman," insisted the watchman doggedly.

"A heap of camel dung!" scoffed the corporal.

"In the middle of the river?" said the watchman angrily.

"Anyway," said Owen, "it's not there now."

"It was there."

"Then what has happened to it?"

"Perhaps," suggested the corporal, "the river has washed it away?"

Owen looked up and down the river. It stretched, broad and placid, to the horizon on both sides. Further on down, near to the city, a single felucca was gliding gracefully in towards the bank. It came to rest and then there was nothing else moving in the intense heat of the late morning Egyptian sun.

He scanned the water's edge carefully. At this time of year, with the flood still some weeks off, the Nile had shrunk back into its bed, uncovering a wide strip of mud, now baked hard and dry and cracked like crazy paving. Far away he thought he could see some goats grazing. But there was no suspicious heap lying grounded in the shallows, no flotsam or jetsam at all. Anything that came ashore would be snatched up at once by thrifty beachcombers.

Under his feet a little floating clump of Um Suf, Mother of Wool, papyrus reed, torn loose from its moorings hundreds of miles to the south, nestled along the bank and came to rest against the shoal. Nestled and stuck. The current was not even sufficient to tug it loose again.

"It can't have!" said the watchman angrily. "It was lying right up on the shoal."

"How did it get there, then?" asked the corporal. "Did it jump up there like a fish?"

This was exactly the kind of non-issue that Owen didn't want to get involved in. In fact, he didn't want to get involved in any of this at all.

"This isn't anything to do with me," he said. "This is not for the Mamur Zapt."

"Quite right, effendi!" said the corporal smartly. "Only a woman."

That was not what he had meant.

"This is a matter for the Parquet," he said.

This was an ordinary crime if ever he'd seen one. And ordinary crimes were handled by the Parquet, the Department of Prosecutions of the Ministry of Justice. The Egyptian legal system was like the French. Conduct of a criminal investigation was the responsibility of a prosecuting lawyer, not of the police. The police worked under his direction. And, of course, when a crime was reported they were the ones who had to notify the Parquet in the first place.

"Has the Parquet been notified?" he said sternly.

The corporal scratched his head.

"I expect so," he said.

"*Expect so?*" Owen boiled over with fury. "I should bloody well expect so, too. And I'd expect them to be here. I'd expect them to be wasting their time on this foolish nonsense and not me. Whose idea was it to send for the Mamur Zapt anyway?"

"I don't know anything about it," said the corporal hurriedly.

"One said that you were near, effendi," said the watchman forlornly, "and the Chief thought—"

Owen knew damned well what the District Chief had thought. He had thought, here was somebody senior he could pass responsibility to without having to do anything about it himself. Right on the spot, too! He wouldn't even have to stir out of the cool of his office. While he, Owen was tearing around all over the place like a bloody lunatic!

"Tell the Chief," he said ominously, "that I'll be wanting a word with him."

This was ridiculous. He couldn't afford to be spending his time here. He had a dozen men on the other side of town waiting for him. They had been about halfway through when the message had come from the District Chief. He had dropped everything and left. And you could bet that the moment he'd left they'd sat down in the shade.

He set off back up the bank.

After a moment's hesitation the other two ran after him. "Effendi! Effendi!"

"You stay here. Wait for the Parquet. You can tell it all to them."

He reached the top of the bank, lizards scattering out of the way in front of him. He was just about to plunge back into the streets when he saw someone running towards him. It was one of the men he had left.

"Effendi!" he gasped. "A message! From the Bimbashi!"

"Yes?"

"You are to go to the river."

Owen looked round. Behind him the river sparkled placidly in the sun. Apart from the corporal and the watchman, there wasn't a soul in sight. Nothing moved on the bank or out on the water. The mud shoal and its hump dozed tranquilly in the heat.

"Well," said Owen, "I'm at the river. But why on earth…?"

ᏉᎢᏁᎯᎾ

The Bimbashi arrived shortly afterwards.

He was in a motorcar. This was impressive since there were relatively few cars in Cairo in 1909 and the police force itself did not boast one. Normally it went about its business either on foot or in an arabeah, the horse-drawn cab distinctive to the city. If it needed a car it borrowed the Army's one.

But that was battered and sober: this one was new and, well, spectacular.

"Green," said the driver of the car, noting with satisfaction Owen's interest. "There was a bit of a fuss about that. The Mufti complained. But I said: 'It's almost the family color, isn't it?'"

The Bimbashi, McPhee, pink and fair and anxious, rushed forward.

"This is Captain Owen, Prince. Owen, Prince Narouz."

"Ah!" said the Prince. "The Mamur Zapt. You got here quickly. Efficient of you. But then"—he smiled ambiguously—"we know the Mamur Zapt to be efficient, don't we?"

He was perhaps in his late, perhaps in his early thirties. All the males of the Khedive's family tended to thicken out and age suddenly as they approached middle age. Owen knew from the title that this was a member of the Egyptian Royal Family but which of the Khedive's numerous progeny it was escaped him for the moment.

The third person in the car was another Egyptian, definitely about thirty, slim and dressed, like the Prince, in a smart, European-style suit but with the usual potlike tarboosh of the Egyptian professional on his head.

Owen knew who this one was. His name was Mahmoud el Zaki and he was one of the Parquet's rising stars. They embraced warmly in the Arab fashion. They had worked together often and got on well.

The Prince and McPhee had walked on to the top of the bank and were standing looking down at the river.

"What's all this about?" whispered Owen.

"Don't know. Someone else was going to do this one and then they suddenly switched me onto it."

They joined the others.

"What's going on?" Owen asked.

McPhee turned a concerned face towards him.

"Something absolutely frightful has happened," he said. "The Prince was on a dahabeeyah last night coming back from Karnak and someone fell overboard."

"A woman?"

McPhee nodded.

"As soon as we got the report we suspected—well, we knew, I suppose. She couldn't swim."

"*You* got the report?"

"The Prince phoned Garvin first thing this morning."

Garvin was the Commandant of the Cairo police force. McPhee was his deputy.

"What about the Parquet?"

"We got the report in the ordinary way," said Mahmoud. "At that stage it was just that a body had been found. I imagine," he said to the Prince, "that you yourself rang up later?"

"After I had spoken to Garvin." The Prince hesitated. "You see, I didn't want this to be…clumsily handled."

"Oh, of course not!" said McPhee sympathetically. "The poor girl! And the family, of course!"

"Yes. And the Khedivial connection."

"Of course. Of course."

"It could be embarrassing, you see. Politically, I mean."

"For you?" asked Owen.

The Prince looked at him coolly.

"For the Khedive. There is no particular reason why it should be. There is nothing, shall I say, to be embarrassed *about*. But you know what the Press is and people are. It could be used. Turned against the Khedive. Used to discredit him. Would the British Government want that, Captain Owen?"

"Assuredly not. The Khedive is a valued friend and ally."

Not only that. He was the façade which concealed the realities of British power in Egypt.

For while the Khedive was the apparent ruler of Egypt, the country's real ruler, in 1909, was the British Consul-General. His rule was indirect and unobtrusive. The Khedive had his Prime Minister, his Ministers and his Ministries. But at the top of each Ministry, alongside each Minister, was a British "Adviser" and all the key public posts were occupied by Englishmen.

Like the Commandant and Deputy Commandant of the Cairo Police.

Like the Mamur Zapt.

"That's what the Consul-General thought too," said the Prince. "I spoke to him this morning."

"We are to give whatever help we can," McPhee told Owen.

"How far does the help extend?" asked Owen.

The Prince smiled.

"Not as far as you are evidently supposing," he said. "I appreciate that someone has died. The matter must be investigated and will be most ably, I am sure, by Mr. el Zaki, here. If a crime has been committed—oh, negligence, say—those responsible must be punished. It's all straight and above board, Captain Owen, and Mr. el Zaki's involvement should be a guarantee of that."

"I have complete confidence in Mr. el Zaki."

"Quite. But, you see, there is the other dimension too. The political one. The case needs to be handled from that point of view too. It needs to be…managed."

"I see. And you would like me to provide that management?"

"Who better?"

Owen could think of lots of people he would prefer to see handling this particular case. Most people, in fact.

The Prince was watching his face.

"It's not as bad as all that," he said. "We're not asking you to do anything you shouldn't. It's mainly a matter of controlling the Press."

"It's not easy to control the Press on something like this. It's bound to get out. In a foreign newspaper, perhaps."

In cosmopolitan Cairo with its three principal working languages and at least a dozen other widely used ones people turned as readily to the overseas press as they did to the native one. More readily, for the former wasn't censored.

"That's why I spoke of…management."

"I see."

"Good!" said the Prince briskly. "Then that's all sorted out."

He looked down at the riverbed below him.

"Well," he said, "I suppose we ought to go down. You'll be needing an identification."

"There's just one thing," said Owen.

෧෩෧

"Not there?" said the Prince incredulously.

"Not there?" echoed McPhee.

Mahmoud did not say anything but started immediately down the slope.

By the time they got there he was already talking to the watchman.

"I don't understand," said the Prince. "Are you saying that this is all a mistake?"

"A body *was* reported," said Owen.

"A false report?"

Owen shrugged.

The watchman fell on his knees.

"It was *true*, effendi," he protested vehemently. "I saw it. I swear it. On my father's…"

"I begin to doubt," said the Prince coldly, "whether you had a father."

The watchman swallowed.

"It was there, effendi," he said, pointing to the shoal. "There! I swear it."

"Then where is it?"

The watchman swallowed again.

"I don't know, effendi," he said weakly. "I don't know."

"The river, effendi," insinuated the corporal *sotto voce*. "It could be the river."

But the Prince had already turned away.

"This is awkward," he said.

"It could have been somebody else," said Owen. "It needn't have been the girl."

"The report was of a woman's body."

"Another woman, perhaps."

The Prince shrugged.

"Unlikely, I would have thought. Unless you have women's bodies floating down this part of the river all the time."

"Oh no, effendi," said the corporal hastily.

"Awkward," said the Prince again. "It would have been much more convenient…Well, it must be somewhere. You'll have to find it, that's all."

"I'll get onto it right away," promised McPhee. "I'll alert the police stations—"

"Quietly," said the Prince. "If that's possible with the police."

"There's a bend below the city," said Mahmoud. "It will probably turn up there."

"Have someone looking out for it," ordered the Prince. "This needs to be handled discreetly." He looked at Owen. "You're managing this. Remember?"

ᘓᴥᑏᑏᘉ

Owen and Mahmoud were left on the riverbed.

"Like it?" said Owen.

"No," said Mahmoud. "But then, there's quite a lot I don't like."

He called the watchman over.

"Come here," he said. "You saw the body. Describe it."

"It was a woman."

"Clothed?"

"Of course!" said the watchman, shocked.

"It mightn't have been. What was she wearing?"

The watchman looked down at his feet, embarrassed.

"Shintiyan," he muttered.

"Trousers?" said the corporal, unable to restrain himself. "Oh ho, Abu, this is the stuff of dreams!"

"Color?"

"Pink," muttered the watchman.

"She was not a village woman, then?"

"No, effendi." The watchman shook his head definitely.

"What else was she wearing? A tob?"

The watchman hesitated.

"I think so, effendi. It was hard to tell."

The corporal guffawed.

"He only saw the shintiyan!"

"She wore something, though, apart from the shintiyan?"

"Oh, yes, effendi. It was just the way she was lying," he said aside to the corporal. "That's how I came to see them."

The shintiyan were ordinary trousers, not undergarments, and came right down to the ankle.

"How was she lying?" asked Mahmoud.

The watchman lay down on the sand and put his arms together over his head. His body formed a kind of crescent.

"There's a hump on the shoal," he said. "She was lying round that."

"Show me."

They splashed out to the shoal. The water was shallow and hardly came up to their knees.

The shoal was some twenty feet long, and about four feet wide. At the downstream end it rose into a little hump.

"She was lying round that," said the watchman. "Head that side, feet this."

"The body probably caught up against it on its way downstream," said Owen.

"Well, yes," said Mahmoud. "Possibly. But you can see from the mud that normally the upper part of the shoal is above the water."

"The wash of a boat? The Prince's boat?"

"Possibly."

Mahmoud examined the mud carefully.

"We'll have to get the trackers out here," he said. "I can't see anything."

"Does it matter?" asked Owen. "If anything happened, it happened on the boat. Where the body finishes up is neither here nor there."

"Yes," said Mahmoud. "Except that there's one thing I find puzzling. I can accept that the body might have been carried high up on to the shoal by an exceptionally heavy wash from a boat. But I find it hard to believe in a second

exceptionally heavy wash from a boat in the same morning—
one so heavy as to carry the body off again."

ᏅᎲᏬ

Owen had to go back to his men. He found them, as he expected,
doing nothing. They were supposed to be carrying out an arms
search. In fact, they were chatting peacefully in the shade.

He put them back to work. The tip had come from a
reliable source. You didn't waste things like that in his
business.

According to his informant, the arms had come into the
quarter the previous day. The consignment was substantial,
at least two donkey-loads. It would be hidden in the quarter
until the necessary deals were struck and the arms could be
distributed.

For a consignment as large as that, hiding places were
limited. The houses in this poor part of town were single-
story, one-room affairs and there was seldom any furniture
in the room. The men would simply come into the room,
stand and look.

Usually they concentrated their attention on the roof. The
roofs were flat and used for storage: onions, maize stalks, cattle
dung being dried out for fuel, firewood.

It was under the firewood that arms were usually hidden.
The men would run up the outside staircase and make straight
for that.

By now, though, the sun was directly overhead and on the
roofs it was unbearably hot. It was hot even to step on them.
The men winced as their bare feet touched the plaster and Owen
could feel the heat even through the soles of his shoes.

That was the trouble about missing a couple of hours. If he
had not been called away it would have been done by now.

The men were beginning to slow down. He went round
chivvying.

Two men were taking a suspiciously long time on a roof.
He went up to see what they were doing.

He had maligned them. They were working. Like many of the roofs, this one had a dovecot. It consisted of large earthenware pots stacked on top of each other on their sides so that the mouths all pointed one way like a battery of guns. The doves flew in at the mouths and made their nests inside.

The trouble was that a number of the birds were inside now and the constables, country boys, were conscientiously taking them out one by one before feeling around inside.

"That's all right," he said. "You don't need to do that."

"You told us to check everything!"

"Yes, but—"

He was forced to admit they were right. It *could* be a possible hiding place. Though only for pistols.

"Don't do them all," he said. "Just try a few. Otherwise you'll be here all day."

"We don't want to miss anything," one of them said, reaching unhurriedly into another pot.

"Yes, but we want to get a move on."

"Sure!" they agreed equably.

They were some of the men he had borrowed from the local District Chief. Out here on the edge of the city life was still close to that of the village and the pace was very different from what it was further in.

He thought it would probably confuse them if he insisted on their moving on. Instead, hoping to expedite matters, he squatted down beside them and gave them a hand.

In the relaxed way of countryfolk, they began to chat.

"Did you find what you wanted over there?" asked one of them, inclining his head in the direction of the river.

Over the houses Owen caught a glimpse of blue.

"No."

"Nor here, either. You're not having much luck this morning, are you?"

"There's still time. If we get a move on," he said pointedly.

"Oh yes. Things usually turn out right in the end."

"Yes, but only if—"

He stopped himself. It was pointless. One of the things he had learned since coming to Egypt was that the country had its rhythms and that if you were going to get anywhere you had to work with them and not against them.

"It was a body," he said, changing tack. "Over there. By the river."

"Oh yes."

"Yes. Or rather, a body was reported. By the time I got there it had gone."

The man laughed.

"Bodies have a way of doing that," he said. "Or at least, on this part of the river they do."

"How's that?"

"Oh well, if you find one, that means more work for the Chief, doesn't it?"

"So he doesn't mind too much if one goes missing?"

"He doesn't mind at all."

"How might they go missing?"

"All sorts of ways," said the man vaguely.

"They might hit a pole, for instance," suggested his friend.

"What?"

The two men laughed, as at a private joke.

"They can hit all sorts of things on their way downriver," said the first man, looking at his friend chidingly.

"But what about when they're washed up?"

"That's when they have to be reported."

The man laughed again.

"Are there people working the bank?"

"How do you mean?"

"On the lookout for things. Things that get washed ashore?"

"Oh yes."

"Regulars?"

"Yes."

"Are they organized? Is there a gang? A society?"

The men looked at each other, then dropped their eyes.

"We wouldn't know about that," they said.

They worked on carefully through the dovecot. When they had finished they patted the dovecot affectionately and climbed back unhurriedly down the stairs.

Owen sat thinking. It was a new possibility. Suppose the body had not been washed away? Suppose it had been interfered with? Suppose somebody had got to it?

◌⟋⟍◌

Owen went to see the District Chief afterwards. He had a thing or two he wanted to tell him. To his surprise, when he reached the office he found the green car drawn up outside and the Prince about to go in.

"Why, Captain Owen!" said the Prince, pausing for him. "How felicitous! I was just making sure that everything was covered."

"Isn't McPhee supposed to be doing that?"

"Of course. But it sometimes helps if you remind key people which side their bread is buttered on, don't you think?"

Owen wondered in what sense the District Chief was key. The District Chief was, in fact, looking rather shaken.

"After all," said the Prince with a wave of his hand, "it's not every day that he gets called on by both Royalty *and* the Head of the Secret Police." He gave Owen a sidelong glance. "He is probably more impressed by the latter, I'm afraid."

"I doubt it, Prince."

"You're his boss, aren't you?"

"No. He comes under Mr. McPhee."

"Not the Mamur Zapt? Don't they all come under the Mamur Zapt?"

"No, Prince. The Mamur Zapt is, well, out to one side."

"You, too? Of course, things have changed. In my grandfather's time the Mamur Zapt used to control everything.

He was the Khedive's right-hand man, you know. The man he relied on to keep him in power."

"I am afraid his scope is a little more restricted these days, Prince."

The title Head of the Secret Police was in any case something of a misnomer. Head of the Political Branch of the CID was the closest British equivalent. Perhaps, too, in army terms—and some considered Egypt an occupied country—Head of Political Intelligence.

"Yes. And in the old days he used to serve the Khedive."

"He still does, Your Highness."

The Prince smiled.

"Well," he said. "I am sure you have business of your own with our friend here. Please don't let me interrupt you."

He walked over to one of the low, shuttered windows and sat on the sill.

"Do carry on."

Owen hesitated.

"Not secret, is it? If it is, I will at once remove myself. Though, as you said a moment ago, you are in a sense one of my servants."

"The Khedive's servants, certainly. No, Your Highness, you are, of course, welcome to stay. I was merely going to ask the Chief why he sent for me this morning."

"But is not that obvious?"

"No, far from it. The proper procedure, you see, when a crime is reported, is to notify the Parquet, not the Mamur Zapt."

"I see. Well, man, answer him. Why did you send for him?"

"The Mamur Zapt was nearby," muttered the Chief.

"Well, that seems reasonable. You *were* nearby. And, by the way, that was very prescient of you."

"Hardly. I was conducting a search for arms."

"Really? In this vicinity? There does seem to be a lot going on in this neighborhood. Arms, you say? Well, I suppose that's important."

"Yes. To the Khedive as well as to me."

"You think so? Yes, I suppose you're right. They're just as likely to be used against us as they are against you. We and the British have a lot in common. We're both unpopular."

"Only with some people, Prince."

"Well, yes. The Nationalists! Very trying people. My father keeps wondering whether to bring them in or keep them out. Bring them in and they want to change things. Keep them out and you deny them the chance to share in our unpopularity. Which is hardly wise, don't you think? I'm all for bringing them in."

"You could always go halfway. Bring them in so that they share the unpopularity but don't give them enough power to change anything."

"Ah yes. Of course, that is the British solution. And very effective, too. But then, what about these guns? These arms of yours? Don't you think there's a danger that if people are disappointed they're more ready to try extreme solutions? What do you do then?"

"Conduct arms searches."

"I see. Why, Captain Owen, you've persuaded me! I am now convinced that your work was very important. Too important to be interrupted. So, fellow, why did you interrupt him?"

The District Chief, who had not altogether followed all this, looked blank.

"I was wondering whether he'd received a phone call," explained Owen. "A phone call to suggest that there were other things more important."

"Oh, me, you mean? No. I always start at the top. I get round to the bottom later. As, of course, you see."

"I was puzzled," said Owen. "The message from the Chief came first. Before the message from Mr. McPhee."

The Prince looked at him sharply.

"Yes," he said, "that *is* interesting." He slipped off the sill, walked across to the Chief and stood in front of him. "That *is* interesting. Well," he said silkily, "*did* you receive a phone call this morning?"

"No," said the Chief, "no phone calls."

"Or any other kind of message?" asked Owen. "Did someone come to see you, for instance?"

"No."

"The Mamur Zapt will check," warned the Prince. "If I were you I'd get it right the first time."

"No one came. There were no messages, effendi. I swear it."

"So why," asked the Prince, "did you send for Captain Owen?"

"I thought—I thought—the Mamur Zapt was near—and—"

"There may be a simple explanation," said Owen. "Laziness."

"Laziness?"

"He heard there was someone senior in the neighborhood and saw it as a golden opportunity to pass on the responsibility."

"But isn't there a difficulty here? You said yourself earlier that you are not his superior, not directly. Yes, and that in any case the normal procedure was for the matter to be reported to the Parquet."

"These are facts of which I meant to remind him."

"I see. Good."

The Prince wheeled away.

"Carry on," he said over his shoulder.

"Another time. Your Highness, I must apologize. I have been delaying you. You yourself had business, I think, with the District Chief?"

"Well, yes. Certainly."

"Don't let me delay you further. Please carry on."

He walked over to the window and sat on the sill.

"Don't mind me," he said encouragingly.

The Prince sat silently for a moment looking at Owen. Then he suddenly smiled.

"*Touché!*" he said. "However, I don't mind you hearing."
He crooked his finger. The Chief came towards him.

"The body that was washed up this morning: I am
interested in it. If I am interested, other people will be, too.
Now. One!" He held up his forefinger. "If anyone comes
round inquiring, I want to know who they are. Two!" He
held up the second finger. "You are to tell them nothing.
They may offer you money. If you take it, I shall hear, and
you know what to expect, don't you? On the other hand, if
you report all to me it may be that *I* shall give you money.
Understand? Three!" He clasped the third finger. "It may be
that you will come across information which you think would
interest me. Information about the body, for instance. Not
about the girl, I don't need that. Just the body. I am prepared
to pay for such information and pay well. Now, have you got
all that?"

"Yes, Your Highness."

"I'm sure you have. But just to make even surer, I am
going to ask you to tell me what the three things are that
could make you rich."

He held up his forefinger and looked questioningly at the
District Chief.

"If people come asking," said the Chief hoarsely.

"You are to say nothing. Good. And the second?"

"I am to tell you who they are."

"Excellent!" The Prince looked at Owen. "The man is well
on his way to becoming rich, wouldn't you say?"

"There are sometimes dangers in trying to get rich too
quickly."

"Oh, pooh! Don't be a spoilsport. The man wants to get
rich. Let him have his dream! Now, fellow, what is the third
thing you have to do?"

He held up the third finger. The Chief kept his eyes fixed
on it.

"To bring you information, Your Highness. Information
about the body."

"Good." The Prince patted him on the back. "Good fellow! You have learned your lesson."

"Thank you, Your Highness."

He seemed uncertain, however.

"Well?" said the Prince. "What is it?"

"I—I—there is a thing I don't quite understand, Your Highness."

"Yes? What is it?"

"The body, Your Highness. You said you wanted information about the body, Your Highness."

"Yes?"

The District Chief hesitated, then took the plunge.

"What sort of information, Your Highness? I will go and see the body if you wish and describe it to you. In detail, naturally. But—"

He looked uncomfortably to Owen for support.

"No, no, no!" said the Prince hastily. "Not that sort of thing!"

"Then—?"

"The body has disappeared," said Owen.

"Disappeared?"

"Gone. From the sandbank where it was apparently found."

"Gone?" said the District Chief, as if he could not believe his ears. "Gone?"

"That's right. When I got there it was gone."

"Abu?" said the Chief faintly. "Ibrahim?"

"We got there together. It had already gone. Ibrahim rather doubted it had been there in the first place."

The Chief unexpectedly went ashen. He bowed his head between his hands.

"God!" he said. "God!"

"I want to find it," said the Prince. "Quickly, and before anyone else does. Got it?"

Chapter 2

Unusually, there was a meeting on the British side about how to handle it. Garvin was there, Commandant of the Cairo Police and Owen's nominal superior; McPhee, Deputy Commandant, earnest, concerned and straightforward—too straightforward by half to be a Cairo policeman and far too straightforward for something like this; Paul, an aide-de-camp of the Consul-General's; and Owen.

The Consul-General usually steered clear of too direct an involvement in Egyptian policing. Garvin reported formally to the Khedive—and the Consul-General was punctilious about the forms. He was particularly careful of any involvement with the Mamur Zapt, which was why Owen not only reported formally to the Khedive but was nominally subordinate to Garvin.

It was, therefore, unusual to have a meeting of this sort. But then, as Paul, chairing the meeting on behalf of the Consul-General, made clear, the circumstances were unusual.

"It's not every day that an heir to the throne gets involved in something like this."

"*Is* he an heir to the throne?"

"One of many. The Khedive has a number of sons and all of them see themselves as potential heirs."

"Where does this one fit in?"

"He is the son of the Khedive's third wife, so not high up in the stakes. On the other hand, his mother is still a favorite of the Khedive's, which is often significant. He is able and energetic, which makes him stand out among the Khedive's progeny. And front runners in a thing of this sort are unfortunately prone to accidents."

"He seemed a bit of a playboy to me," said McPhee.

"That car, of course. But look at it another way: as an indication of Narouz's interest in things modern and things Western."

"I see."

"Yes. I thought you would. The Consul-General, and Al-Lurd before him, see him as a man England could do business with."

Al-Lurd was Lord Cromer, the man who had run Egypt for over twenty years before the present incumbent. If two such people, the one popular with Conservatives, the other a nominee of the new Liberal government in London, took that view, the Prince had a lot going for him.

"It would be unfortunate," said Paul, "if he were to be derailed at this point."

There was a little silence.

"Is that a directive?" asked Owen.

"A hint, rather. Call it: putting you in the picture. Alerting you to the position of His Majesty's Government."

"As strong as that?" said Garvin.

"I can relax it a bit, provided you've got the general idea. If he's done anything *really* wicked I don't think HMG would be prepared to go out on a limb on his behalf. There are, after all, other possible candidates. But if it's only mildly wicked we would feel it a pity to be too legalistic."

"What counts as only mildly wicked?"

"I don't think I'd like to give you a general answer. These things have to be decided in the light of circumstances."

"I'm not sure I find that very helpful," said Garvin. "What exactly is to be our position?"

"Aloof," said Paul. "Aloof, but watching."

"Not get too close to it? Well, that's probably sensible."

"Should be manageable," said Garvin. "After all, it's Parquet business really."

"Quite. The police will assist the Parquet and work under their direction as usual. But that's at the local level. There's no need for senior involvement."

"I quite agree," said Garvin. "No point in that at all."

No fool he.

"McPhee's involved already," said Owen.

"I think he can drop out now."

"The Prince thinks he's involved."

"The Prince, I believe, has changed his mind."

"Since yesterday?"

"Yes."

"I see."

Someone else been making telephone calls?

"I think that's very reasonable," said Garvin. "McPhee's got enough demands on his time already. When all is said and done, this is just a straightforward crime and we wouldn't normally put him on to something like this."

"We don't even know it is a crime," Paul pointed out.

"No, no, of course not," said Garvin, hurriedly changing tack. "Could be just an accident."

"It's for the Parquet to decide how it wants to treat it. Crime or accident."

He looked at Owen.

"They've put Mahmoud on to it, haven't they?"

"Yes."

"How will he play it?"

"Straight."

"Mahmoud's a good chap," said McPhee.

"Mahmoud's going to have to take some hard decisions," said Paul.

He finished his coffee.

"Which brings me to the final thing we need to discuss. You asked me about the stance we were to adopt. I said aloof. I also said watching."

"We wouldn't want it to go wrong," said Garvin.

"We couldn't afford for it to go wrong. We've got to have someone in there."

"I thought you said you didn't want any senior involvement?"

"Overt. No overt involvement at the senior level."

Another little silence.

"This is hardly straightforward policing," said Garvin slowly. "I would say it was more—political."

"You said it *was* straightforward policing a moment ago. When you wanted to shift it to the Parquet."

"A straightforward crime. Not straightforward policing. There are other dimensions here. Political ones."

"I think Owen's the chap," said Paul.

"I don't like it."

"Who does?"

"I'm not going to get involved in any cover-up."

"I don't think Owen should be asked to cover up anything," said McPhee.

"We're not asking him to. Not yet, anyway. And I don't think it need come to that, not if it's handled in the right way. With a bit of dexterity, I mean. The Press, the politicians, the Prince himself. Mahmoud. The Khedive, too, perhaps."

"It's a tall order."

"I've every confidence in the boy," said Paul, watching him.

"I still don't like it. I'm not going to get involved in any covering up."

"I hope it won't be necessary. But this is politics. You know, you policemen are lucky. If you meet a bad guy, you lock him up. If I meet a bad guy I usually have to shake hands with him and do a deal."

"I'm not shaking hands," said Owen.

Paul smiled.

"You're in politics now," he said, "whether you like it or not. And I think you'll find you're going to have to take some hard decisions. Like Mahmoud."

ᓍᙏᙏᙅ

"And, of course, there was the harem," said the eunuch.

"The harem?" said Owen, startled.

"The Prince always travels with one."

"Even to Luxor?" asked Mahmoud.

"Certainly to Luxor. The Prince has an estate there."

"And that's where he had been this time?"

"Yes."

They were sitting in the cabin of the dahabeeyah. It was a modern one, specially fitted out for the Prince, and had windows. Through the window beside him Owen could see a large rat sunning itself on a mooring rope.

"I had gathered the impression that the Prince had intended to be away only for a few days," said Mahmoud.

"That is true."

"How long did he spend at the estate?"

"Two days."

"Only two days? That is a very short time, especially when you have to travel all that way."

"The Prince does not like his estate."

"He was principally interested in seeing Luxor, then?"

"The Prince does not like Luxor, either."

"What does he like?" asked Owen.

"Cannes."

In the old days, before the advent of Mr. Cook's steamers, when tourists used to sail down to Luxor by dahabeeyah, the port had been full of the old-fashioned, native sailing craft. The tourist would come and choose one. It would then be towed across the river and sunk—temporarily. This was to get rid of the rats. The trick was, though, to sail away

immediately that dahabeeyah had been raised. Otherwise it
would be reinfested—along the ropes—at once.

"What, then, was the purpose of his visit?" asked Mahmoud.

The eunuch shrugged.

"I wouldn't have thought the Prince was one to wish to
spend a week admiring the beauties of the riverbank."

"The Prince spent his time in the cabin playing cards with
the Prince Fahid."

"Ah? The Prince Fahid was on the boat, too?"

"Yes."

"Had he, too, brought his harem?"

"The Prince Fahid is too young to have a harem."

"He is Prince Narouz's son?"

"Nephew."

"The Prince was perhaps showing him the sights?"

"What sights?"

"Luxor?"

"The Prince is not interested in antiquities."

"What, then, was the point of the journey?"

"I don't know. Perhaps you had better ask the Prince."

Mahmoud sighed. He had warned Owen beforehand to
expect this. The Prince's entourage wouldn't say anything.
He was finding it difficult to extract even the names of the
people who had been on the dahabeeyah.

"Let us go back to the harem," he said. "How many wives
has the Prince?"

"Four."

"And they were all there with him?"

"Except Latfi, who is having a baby."

"Three, then. There were three in the harem quarters?"

"You spoke of wives only."

"There were others, then? How many?"

"Seven."

"Can you give me their names?" said Mahmoud, taking
out a pencil and notebook.

"I am afraid not."

"Are you sure? You knew Latfi's name."

"I know all their names. But it would not be proper for me to tell you the names of His Highness's wives and concubines."

"But I need to know! I am conducting an investigation!"

"That's as may be, but a man's harem is his own affair."

"Not when part of it disappears overboard."

"What do you mean?"

"You know very well what I mean," said Mahmoud, exasperated. "I told you! His Highness has reported that a passenger on the dahabeeyah with him—"

"But she wasn't in the harem."

"She wasn't?"

"No!"

"What was she doing on board, then?"

"Well…" The eunuch hesitated.

"You may speak," said Owen encouragingly. "Mr. el Zaki puts these questions with the knowledge and agreement of His Highness," possibly stretching the truth a little.

"She was helping to entertain the princes."

"Helping?"

"There were two others. They came on board at Beni Suef."

"On the way up to Luxor or on the way back?"

"On the way up."

"Have you any objection to telling me *their* names?"

"I don't know their names," said the eunuch.

The incident had happened on the return journey. The dahabeeyah had moored for the night and the three girls had been up on the top deck enjoying the evening breeze. They had stayed up there with the princes until it had become dark, early, of course, in Egypt.

Prince Narouz, bored, had descended first. About half an hour later, according to the eunuch, Prince Fahid had followed him, accompanied, possibly reluctantly, by two of the girls. The third had remained on the top deck.

And it was from the top deck, apparently, that she had disappeared. Late, quite late, someone had called up to her, asking when she was going to come down. Sometime after, not having received a reply, they had sent the eunuch to fetch her. He had found the top deck empty.

At first he had assumed that she had climbed down to the lower deck and gone forward. Some members of the crew had been sitting in the bows and it was only when they denied having seen her that he began to search seriously.

"The steersman?" said Mahmoud. "Surely the steersman must have seen?"

On a dahabeeyah the steersman was placed aft, immediately behind the cabin. He usually stood on a little platform raised high enough to enable him to see over and past the cabins when the boat was moving.

After the boat had stopped for the night there was always some work still to be done on the platform. The rudder bar had to be lashed and the ropes stowed. The eunuch said, however, that the steersman had finished his work and gone forward before all this happened.

The eunuch had made a cursory search and then had reported the matter to Prince Narouz. Narouz had been angry, first with the girl for playing the fool and then with the eunuch for not finding her.

He had searched the boat himself. Gradually he came to realize that something was seriously amiss.

By now, of course, it was dark and hard to see anything on the water. The Prince had had all the men up on deck scanning the river with the aid of oil lamps. Meanwhile the eunuch had been concluding a search below.

When he had gone up on deck again he found that the Prince had lowered two small rowing boats and was systematically scouring the river. This had continued all night. As soon as it was light the dahabeeyah had sailed downriver with everyone on deck keeping an eye out. They had seen nothing.

In the end they had abandoned the search, set the Prince down so that he could report the incident at once, and sailed on to Bulak.

"I shall need to speak to the Ship's Captain, the Rais," said Mahmoud. "Also to the crew. One by one. Also to the servants. Those girls, of course. Then the harem."

"The harem!" said the eunuch, shocked. "Certainly not! What sort of boat do you think this is?"

෴

The dahabeeyah was moored across the river from the main port. This was the traditional mooring place for dahabeeyahs and in the old days, before Mr. Cook had come with his steamers, there would have been over two hundred of them nudging the bank. They were the traditional way for the rich to travel by water—and in Egypt everyone traveled by water. The Nile was the main, the only, thoroughfare from north to south and the dahabeeyah was its Daimler.

It was a large, flat-bottomed sailing boat rather like a Thames barge or, as tourists were overprone to comment, a College houseboat, except that its cabins were all above deck and all aft. This gave it a weird, lopsided look and might have made it unstable had that not been compensated for by putting the hold forward.

From the point of view of the tourist the arrangement had an additional delight. There was a railed-off space on top of the cabins which served as a kind of open-air lounge, sufficiently high to allow passengers both to enjoy the breeze and to see over the bank. This was important, as in some stretches of the river Mr. Cook's customers might not otherwise have benefited from the remarkable views he had promised them.

Owen himself rather enjoyed the views but he had been a little surprised to learn that they had also drawn the Prince.

"*How* long was he up there?" he asked the Rais, the Ship's Captain, disbelievingly.

"Two hours."

"Of course, it was cool up there."

"Yes."

"And he was keeping the woman company."

"They were already up there," said the Rais. There was a note of disapproval in his voice.

"Really? By themselves?"

Mahmoud clucked sympathetically.

"By themselves."

"That's not right!"

"They shouldn't have been up there at all!" said the Rais. "There's a place for women. And it's the harem."

"Ah, but these weren't—I mean, they weren't properly in the Prince's harem."

"They ought to have been. And they ought to have stayed there."

"Were they flaunting themselves?" asked Mahmoud, commiserating.

The Rais hesitated.

"It was enough to be there, wasn't it? My men could hardly take their eyes off them."

"Unseemly!" said Mahmoud.

"It wasn't proper," said the Rais. "The Prince should have known better. Though it is not for me to say that."

"Have you captained for him before?"

"He's never been on the river before. At least, as far as I know."

"So you didn't know what to expect?"

"All he told us was that he wanted to go up to Luxor. With the Prince Fahid. He was very particular about that. The Prince had his own room, of course, and Narouz wanted a cabin next to him. He didn't even want to be with the harem."

"Strange! And then, of course, there were those other women."

"He didn't say anything about them. Not until we were nearly at Beni Suef."

"They were foreigners, weren't they?"

"I'm not saying anything."

"They must have been. Our women wouldn't have behaved like that."

"Indecent!"

"Did they wear veils?"

"They wore veils," the Rais conceded grudgingly. "But they showed their ankles!"

"Oh!" said Mahmoud, shocked.

"How could Hassan be expected to steer when they were flaunting their ankles in front of him?"

"Impossible," Mahmoud agreed. "Impossible!"

They were standing in the stern of the vessel looking up at the back of the cabins. The steersman's platform, with the huge horizontal rudder bar he used for steering, was right beside them.

"But I don't understand!" said Mahmoud. "The woman who stayed up there alone—"

"Shameless!" said the Rais.

"Shameless!" agreed Mahmoud. "But she was right in front of him. Surely he would have seen if she had—well, fallen off."

"Ah, but it was dark, you see. We had stopped for the night."

"So the steersman wasn't there?"

"No."

"Where was he?"

"I don't know," said the Rais. "You'd better ask him."

⟨≈⟩

"And where were you?" asked Mahmoud.

"I was up here," said the steersman. "We'd finished for the day, so I tied the rudder and then came up forward."

They were sitting in the shade of the cook's galley. It was a small shed, rather like a Dutch oven in shape, set well up into the prow to remove it as far as possible from the passengers' cabins. The cook stood up on the forward side, so that the shed protected him when there was a favorable wind. They could hear him there now.

The spot was clearly a favorite one with the crew and there had been several men dozing there when Owen and Mahmoud had appeared. They had gone aft to leave them to talk to the steersman in private, but one of them, the cook presumably, had disappeared into the galley.

"She was still up there at that point?"

"Yes." The steersman's wrinkled face broke into a smile. "I reckoned the midges would soon drive her down."

"It was dark by then?"

"Just. They were up there admiring the sunset but I wanted to stop while there was still a bit of light. There are one or two things you have to do and you can always do them better if you can see what you're doing. Besides, the Prince didn't want us to go too far. He wanted another night on the river!"

"Oh, he did, did he? And why was that?"

"Why do you think? Perhaps he likes it better on the water."

"That's what it was about, you think?"

"What else could it be? He goes down to his estate and doesn't stay there a moment, we call in at Luxor and he doesn't want to go ashore. We go straight down and straight back and the only thing we stop for is to pick up some women at Beni Suef!"

"Those women," said Mahmoud, "what were they like?"

"Classy. But not the sort you'd want to take home with you."

"Foreign."

The steersman hesitated. "Well," he said, "I don't know. Two of them were, certainly. The other—that's the one who finished up in the river—I'm not sure about."

"You're sure about the others, though?"

"Oh yes. You could hear them talking. Mind you, she was talking with them. I don't know, of course, but it just seemed to me...well, and then there were the clothes."

"What about the clothes?"

"Well, they all wore the tob." The tob was a loose outer gown. "And the burka, of course." The burka was a long face veil which reached almost to the ground. "But from where I was you could see their legs."

"Yes. The Rais told us."

"I'll bet he did! He oughtn't to have seen that, ought he? I mean, he wouldn't have noticed if he hadn't been looking. You'd have thought a man like that, strict, he's supposed to be—"

"The women," said Mahmoud patiently.

"Yes, well, the thing was that—I mean, I couldn't see clearly—but I reckon those two had European clothes on underneath their tobs. You could see their ankles. But the other one, well, I caught a glimpse. She was wearing shintiyan."

"Pink ones?" said Owen.

"Why, yes," said the steersman, surprised. "That's right. How did you know? Oh, I suppose you've seen the body."

"Never mind that," said Mahmoud. "Let's get back to when she was on the top deck. She was up there when you last saw her?"

"Yes."

"Alone?"

"Yes."

"Why didn't she go down with the others?"

"I don't know."

"Had they been quarreling?"

"I don't know."

"You heard them talking."

"Well, it was not so much quarreling. I think the Prince was trying to get her to do something. Like, persuade her."

"And she didn't want to?"

"I couldn't really tell," confessed the steersman. "I couldn't understand the language, see? It was just the impression I got. He wasn't nasty or anything, not even angry, really. He was just trying—well, to persuade her, like I said."

"He didn't get anywhere, though?"

"No."

"How was she? I mean, was *she* angry?"

"I couldn't really say. You never know what's going on behind those burkas. You think all's going well and the next moment—bing! They've hit you with something. My wife's like that."

"Were there any tears?"

"Tears? Well, I don't know. Not so much tears but you know how they get sometimes, you think they're going to cry and they don't, they just keep going on and on. A bit like that."

"With the Prince? When he was trying to persuade her?"

"Yes. And with the girls, too. A bit earlier. Going on and on."

"Did they get fed up with her?"

"They left her alone after a bit. Then the Prince came up and had a try and he didn't do any better." He broke off. "Is this helping?" he asked.

"Yes."

"Good. I like to help. Only—all this talking!" He suddenly pounded on the back of the galley with his fist.

"What's the matter?" asked the cook, sticking his head out.

"How about some tea? I'm so dry I can't speak."

"It sounded to me as if you were doing all right. I'd have brought you some before only I didn't want to interrupt you."

He placed a little white enamel cup before each of them and filled it with strong black tea.

"No sugar," he said. "You'd think we'd have sugar on board the Prince's dahabeeyah but we don't."

"It's that eunuch," said the steersman. "The stuff never even gets here."

"It goes somewhere else, does it?" asked Mahmoud sympathetically.

"Into his pocket!" said the steersman.

Mahmoud looked up at the cook.

"You were here that night, weren't you? The night the girl disappeared?"

"Yes. I was just making supper when that stupid eunuch came along making a great commotion."

"You left the girl there," Mahmoud said to the steersman, "and then you came along here. Did you have a cup of tea at that point?"

"Yes," said the steersman, "I always have one when I finish."

"Tea first, then supper," said the cook.

"And you had a cup with him, perhaps?"

"I did. I always do."

"Here? Sitting here?"

"Yes. Several of us."

"And you were still sitting here when the eunuch came?"

"*I* was," said the steersman.

"I had just got up," said the cook. "To make the supper."

"So whatever it was that happened," said Mahmoud, "happened while you were sitting here."

"I suppose so," said the steersman. "Well, it must have."

"Yes, it must have. And you still say you saw nothing? Heard nothing?"

"Here, just a minute—!"

"We weren't looking!"

"We were talking!"

"You would have seen a person. Or—"

"We didn't see anything!"

"Two people. On the cabin roof. Together."

"Here!" said the steersman, scrambling to his feet. "What are you saying?"

"I'm asking," said Mahmoud. "Did you see two people?"

"No!"

"Up there together. Whoever they were."

"I didn't see anything!"

"None of us saw anything!"

"Thirty feet away and you saw nothing?"

"We weren't looking!"

"You took care not to look."

"We were talking!"

"And nothing attracted your attention? Someone is attacked—"

"Attacked!"

"Or falls. And you know nothing about it? If she'd jumped into the water she'd have made a splash."

"A splash? Who hears a splash? There are splashes all the time."

"One as big as this? You are boatmen. You would have heard."

"Truly!" said the steersman. "I swear to God—"

"He hears what you say!" Mahmoud warned him.

"And sees all that happens. I know. Well, he may have seen what happened to the girl but I didn't."

The steersman showed them off the boat. At the gangway he hesitated and then ran up the bank after them.

"What was it, then? *Was* she knocked on the head?"

"I don't know," said Mahmoud.

"I thought you'd seen the body?"

"No. It's not turned up yet."

"Oh." He seemed disappointed. Then he brightened. "Tell you what," he said, "I know where it will fetch up, more than likely."

"Yes?"

The steersman pointed downriver to where men were working on a scaffolding which stretched out across the river.

"See that? That's the new Bulak bridge. That's where they finish up these days."

༄

They were sharing the boat with a kid goat, a pile of onions and the boatman's wife, who sat, completely muffled in tob and burka, as far away from them as was possible.

It had been the steersman's idea. They had been about to set out for the main bridge when he had said:

"Are you going back to Bulak? Why don't you get Hamid to run you over?"

He had pointed along the bank to where an elderly Arab was standing in the water bent over the gunwale of a small, crazily-built boat. The sides were not so much planks as squares of wood stuck on apparently at hazard. The sail was a small, tattered square sheet.

"In that? I don't think so," said Owen.

But Mahmoud, fired with enthusiasm for the life marine, was already descending the bank.

With the two of them on board, the stern dipped until the gunwale was inches above the water. The bows, with the woman and the goat, rose heavenward. The boatman inspected this critically for a moment, but then, unlike Owen, seemed satisfied.

He perched himself on the edge of the gunwale and took the two ends of the rope in his hands. One he wedged expertly between his toes. The other he wound round his arm.

The wind caught the sail and he threw himself backwards until the folds of his galabeah were trailing in the water. The boat moved comfortably out into the river.

Now they were in midstream they could see the new bridge more clearly. There were workmen on the scaffolding and, down at the bottom, a small boat nudging its way along the length of the works.

The boatman pointed with his head.

"That's the police boat," he said. "It comes every day to pick up the bodies."

"Can you take us over there?" asked Mahmoud.

The boatman scampered across to the opposite gunwale, turned the boat, turned it again and set off on a long glide which took them close in along the bridge.

"Bring us in to the boat," said Mahmoud.

A tall man in the police boat looked up, saw Mahmoud and waved excitedly.

"Ya Mahmoud!" he called.

"Ya Selim!" answered Mahmoud warmly.

A couple of policemen caught the boat as it came in alongside and steadied it. Mahmoud and the other man embraced affectionately.

"Why, Mahmoud, have you done something sensible at last and joined the river police?"

"Temporarily; this is my boat."

Selim inspected it critically.

"The boatman's all right," he said, "but I'm not so sure about the boat."

He shook hands with the boatman.

"Give me your money," said the boatman, "and I'll have a boat as good as yours."

"And the Mamur Zapt," said Mahmoud.

Selim shook hands again and gave him a second look.

"I don't think we've met," said Owen.

"No. I've met Mahmoud, though. We were working on a case last year." He looked at them again. "The Mamur Zapt *and* the Parquet," he said. "This must be important."

"It's the girl," said Mahmoud. "You've received notification, I'm sure."

"Pink shintiyan? That the one?"

"That's the one."

"Not come through yet. When did it happen?"

"The night before last. About three miles upstream."

"She'll have sunk, then. Otherwise she'd have come through by now."

Owen looked out along the works. There seemed a lot of water passing through the gaps.

"Could she have gone through and missed you?"

"She could. But most of them finish up against the scaffolding. In the old days before we started building the bridge they used to fetch up on a bend about two miles down.

That was better for us because it's in the next district and meant they had to do the work and not us."

"Ah, but that meant they missed all the glory, too!"

"I think the average Chief would prefer to do without the glory!"

Owen laughed. "We've known a few like that!"

"Yes. We sometimes get the feeling that not all the bodies that come down to us need have done."

"You think so?"

"Sure of it."

"It's important to pick up this one," said Mahmoud.

"Yes, I'm checking them myself. We've had two women through this week. One of them's old and one of them's young, but I don't think the young one could be the one you're looking for, not unless she changed her trousers on the way down."

"The trousers is about all we've got at the moment. I hope to add some details later. Keep the young one just in case."

"It'll be some time before she's traced and identified anyway. They don't always come from the city. Sometimes it's a village upstream."

"Well, keep her. Just on the off chance."

"If she's sunk, what then?" asked Owen.

"Oh, she'll come up. Gases. In the body. It'll take a day or two. Then the body comes up and floats on down to us. We get them all in the end."

"I hope you get this one."

They pushed off. Their boat was now downwind and they had to tack. The boatman tucked up the skirts of his galabeah, hooked his knees over the gunwale and leaned far back over the side. Owen, more confident of his transport now, trailed a hand over the side and turned his face to catch the breeze. Beside him, Mahmoud, hands clasped behind head, was thinking.

In the bows the boatman's wife sat muffled from head to foot, invisible behind her veil, anonymous.

Chapter 3

"Does this girl have a name?" demanded Zeinab.

They were lying on cushions in her *appartement*. Very few single women in Cairo had an *appartement* of their own, but Zeinab was rich enough and imperious enough and independent enough to insist on one.

The richness and imperiousness came from her father, Nuri Pasha, not quite one of the Khedive's family but certainly one of his confidants, not exactly trusted—the Khedive, wisely, trusted nobody—but regularly called upon when the Khedive was reshuffling the greasy pack of his Ministers. Nuri was one of Egypt's great landowners and the Khedive considered there was sufficient identity of interest between them for him to be able to use Nuri's services without fear.

Zeinab was Nuri's daughter: illegitimate, but that, as he explained, was not his fault. Her mother had been a famous courtesan, doted on by all Cairo but in particular by Nuri, who, though a mature man, had taken the reckless step of proposing that she become his wife and a member of his harem.

Unaccountably, the lady had refused. She was more than willing—since Nuri was handsome as well as rich—to extend him her embraces; but enter his harem? She was a fiercely proud, independent woman and these qualities had passed in more than abundant measure to her daughter.

Nuri had gained his way on one thing. Their child had been acknowledged as his daughter and raised in his house, which gave her all the privileges and benefits of belonging to one of Egypt's leading families. While, admittedly, these were not normally conspicuous in the case of women, for Zeinab they were substantial.

Like most of the Egyptian upper classes, Nuri was a Francophile. He spoke French by preference, read French books and newspapers and followed French intellectual and cultural fashions rather than Egyptian ones. The culture of educated Egyptians was, anyway, in many respects as much French as it was Egyptian. Mahmoud, for instance, had been educated as a lawyer in the French tradition. The Parquet was French through and through.

Zeinab had been brought up in this culture. Her father, finding in her many of the qualities he had admired in her mother, had given her far greater freedom from the harem than was normal and from childhood she had sat in on the political and intellectual discussions her father had with his cronies. She came to share many of his interests and tastes and as she grew up she became something of a companion to him.

All this made Zeinab an interesting woman but a rather unusual one. Men found her formidable and she advanced into her twenties, long past the usual marrying age, without Nuri having received a suitable offer. He began to think of this as a problem.

It was a problem, however, which Zeinab herself solved. She moved out and set up her own establishment. Nuri, though advanced in his thinking, was rather shocked by this. Shocked but intrigued: was Zeinab taking after her mother?

Zeinab, however, was merely following up some of the ideas she had met in her father's own circle. Among his friends were some writers and artists who formed a somewhat Bohemian set. Zeinab, who had strong musical interests, found their company congenial and enjoyed their artistic debates. This talk, too, was very much influenced by French fashions and preoccupations; and from it Zeinab acquired the notion that it was possible for a single woman to set up house on her own.

She did this and enjoyed it and gradually her father and his friends came to accept it; indeed, not even, any longer, to notice it. And she was living like this when she met Owen.

The intensity of their relationship surprised them both. Zeinab, alarmed at herself, backed off a little and insisted on maintaining an independent life while she was working out how to handle all this. Owen, equally alarmed, was content to let it rest like that while he tried to see a way through the likely complications. Neither of them was getting very far.

Meanwhile they carried on as they were and that went very well. They met every day, usually in Zeinab's *appartement* and Zeinab kept a proprietorial eye on what Owen was doing when he was away from her.

"Of course she has a name," he said. "It's just that we haven't found it yet."

"It was the way you were talking," said Zeinab.

"Well, it all sounds pretty anonymous, I know—"

"Yes."

"Until we find out more about her, it's bound to be."

"I just ask myself," said Zeinab, "what kind of woman is likely to be found on Narouz's dahabeeyah."

"And what answer do you get?"

"Someone like me."

"What nonsense! What absolute nonsense!"

It disturbed him.

"Nonsense!" he repeated vehemently.

"It's got to be someone like me, hasn't it? It can't be an ordinary girl from an ordinary family because in Egypt ordinary girls are never allowed to be seen. Not even by their husbands, until after they are married."

"An 'ordinary' girl, as you put it, wouldn't get anywhere near a son of the Khedive."

"No, it would have to be someone from a family of rank, wouldn't it? Like mine?"

"The same thing applies to them. They're kept out of sight, too. More, even, since they know what the Khedive's sons are like. I've been in Egypt four years and I've never seen a Pasha's wife or daughter."

"Except me."

"You're different. You're not at all ordinary. In fact," said Owen, his mind beginning to stray onto a quite different tack, "you're altogether extraordinary—"

But Zeinab refused to be diverted.

"It would be someone like me," she said. "Someone whose family is rich enough for her to meet the Khedive. Someone whose father is, well, modern enough not to care. Someone who's struck out on her own. Someone who's vulnerable."

Unexpectedly she began to cry.

Owen was taken aback. Zeinab cried frequently at the opera, never, up till now, anywhere else. He took her in his arms.

"For Christ's sake!" he said. "You don't even know the girl!"

"I can feel!" sobbed Zeinab. "I can feel!"

"You can get misled by feeling."

Zeinab pulled herself away. "You don't have any feeling," she said, looking at him stormily. This was, however, more like the Zeinab he knew and he felt reassured.

"Aren't you missing out the most likely possibility?" he said. "That she's foreign?"

"I thought you said—?"

"It's what the steersman said. He thought she was different from the other two and they were certainly foreign. Well, she might have been different but still foreign. And isn't that the most likely thing? You don't get the Egyptian women on their own either on the Prince's boat or off it. He's used to mixing with foreign women. Someone he's met at Cannes? I'd have thought it was pretty likely. After all, the Khedive himself—"

"Well, of course," said Zeinab, sniffing, "that's true."

"It was the clothes, you see, that made him think she was Egyptian. The shintiyan."

"*Would* a Frenchwoman wear shintiyan?" asked Zeinab, who herself dressed à la Parisienne. "I certainly wouldn't."

"Maybe to please the Prince. Or as a joke or something."

Zeinab thought it over.

"The other two were foreign, weren't they?"

"Yes. And that's another thing. My guess is that they were from some cabaret or other. That's where he might have come across them. You see, you said the girl would have to come from a family of rank. Well, I don't think girls who let themselves get picked up en masse off the bank to spend a week with a bloke on a dahabeeyah *are* likely to be that high class. Foreign, not too classy, three at a time—that sounds like cabaret to me."

"No decent Egyptian woman would let herself be subjected to such a thing," said Zeinab, removing Owen's hand.

"So," said Owen, putting it back, "they must either be foreign or—"

"Or what?" asked Zeinab.

"Indecent Egyptian women," said Owen, putting his other arm round her.

༺☙

In front of him was a beautiful old building, very like a small mosque with its domes, its façade of red and white stones intermixed, its ornate paneling and intricate arabesques. It was not, however, a mosque but a hammam, a public bathhouse.

The entrance was narrow and below street level. A towel hung over the door.

Owen's men looked at him inquiringly.

The towel meant that the baths were temporarily occupied by women.

"Leave it," said Owen resignedly. The men moved on. Owen made a note to return to the hammam later when the towel had been taken down.

It was not, however, a good start.

He was conducting yet another search of the quarter. His informant swore blind that the arms were still there. He had even been able to specify a little more precisely the area where he thought they were concealed. They were, he said, somewhere near the souk.

The souk was not located, as markets usually were, in a square of its own but occupied the space created by a crossroads. Its stalls spread over the whole area; successfully restricting passage in any direction. Fortunately, this far out of town, there were very few vehicles to pass. The occasional horse cart laden with stones, the occasional handcart carrying ice, were the closest approximation. The Souk Al-Gadira existed only for its immediate neighborhood.

The stalls were erected and dismantled every day so there was little likelihood of the arms being hidden beneath them. They were far more likely to be concealed in one of the buildings round about and it was here that Owen was concentrating the search.

They had gone through the buildings when they had searched the area previously but on that occasion, as Owen reminded himself crossly, he had been summoned away in the middle by that foolish District Chief and sent on that wild goose chase down to the river.

There would be no repetition of that today, he told himself grimly. He would make damned sure they stuck with it and did the job properly.

Only it was not quite so straightforward. First, there had been the hammam. And now, at the end of the street, just ahead of him, was a mosque.

Again the men looked at him inquiringly. And again he hesitated.

Even the Mamur Zapt entered mosques on police business with caution. It was so easy for minister and congregation to get excited. The smallest thing would set them going. The sight of a Western face was enough.

Well, he could do something about that. He needn't go in himself, just send the men in.

Just send the men in? The police were only slightly more *grata* than himself. They were seen as the agents of either an alien, infidel force (the British) or a dissolute secular power (the Khedive). In either case they were unwelcome. It needed only one irascible minister to take umbrage at some fancied slight or misdemeanor for there to be trouble.

"Leave it," he said again. If there was trouble he'd have to spend the rest of the day putting it down and wouldn't be able to get on with the arms search at all.

But this was ridiculous! First, the hammam and now this! This wasn't a search at all. Suppose the arms were hidden inside? And there would be no coming back to the mosque!

He called the men back.

"You two," he said, picking on men he had brought with him from headquarters and therefore more experienced, "you go in and walk through, keeping your eyes open. Don't cause any trouble and don't insist if they look like objecting. Just see what you can see and come back and tell me."

The men nodded and went off. After a while they returned. One of them spread his hands, palms upward, and shrugged.

"OK," said Owen. "Worth a try. Get after the others."

At least it hadn't created uproar.

He moved on up the street, or would have moved on if he had been able to. The street was one of those which led into the souk and its lower end was completely blocked by stalls. Regardless of the general press of humanity, a funeral procession was attempting to pass down it from the other end. Processions, like deaths, were extremely common in Cairo and everyone stopped to look, including Owen, who was a little surprised to see a funeral so early in the day. Usually they took place in the evening when it was cooler.

As funerals went, this was a very medium affair. First came the Yemeneeyeh, six poor men, mostly blind, proceeding two and two, and chanting mournfully, "There is no God but

God." Then there were male relations of the deceased, few in this case. Next came four schoolboys, one of them carrying an open copy of the Koran placed upon a kind of platform of palm sticks and covered with an embroidered kerchief. As they walked, they sang: in rather more sprightly tones than the Yemeneeyeh. And then came the bier, its front draped with a shawl to indicate that it carried a woman, which perhaps accounted for the general meagerness of the proceedings.

All the Cairo world loved a good funeral and the bystanders stopped what they were doing, not so much to let the procession pass but to join in the fun. But where were the dervishes, the munshids, with their singing and dancing and flag-waving? There was admittedly a fiki but he was very restrained and seemed anxious to keep himself invisible at the back. This was a poor affair indeed. Even the female mourners, who followed the bier, were few in number and boringly subdued.

Disappointed, the crowd resumed its business. Which, of course, brought the procession to a halt. Owen cursed and tried to wriggle his way round, failed and had to cut across in front of the donkeys laden with bread and water to give to the poor at the tomb. The poor, judging from the size of the loads, would benefit handsomely.

Once past, Owen hurried to catch up with his men. He fell in alongside two of them at the end of the street. They were the two he had talked to on the previous search, the ones who had been taking such pains with the dovecot.

"Found that body yet?" one of them asked.

"No."

"You won't, either."

Owen stepped aside to let a water carrier pass with his heavy bags.

"Why not?" he asked.

"It's the river. Full of tricks."

"It'll come up sometime."

"Ah yes. But where?"

"Most of them finish up against the bridge these days, apparently."

"Perhaps this one will too. When it gets there."

Owen didn't quite understand this and would have asked more but the two men ducked into the next house. He continued slowly along the street, noting how long it took them. Everything was going to be under control this time.

There was nothing wrong with the efforts of his men at the moment. They were working through the buildings quickly and, as far as he could tell, efficiently.

They turned up the next street. It contained some taller buildings with shops on the ground floor. This would take them longer. After waiting a little, Owen sauntered on.

Halfway up the street was a tall sebil, or fountain house. It was, like the hammam, an old building, clearly predating the other buildings since the street curved back specially to accommodate it.

It was a delightful building. Its totally curved sides were fenced with grilles of exquisite metalwork and its upper story was graciously arcaded. There was a little parapet going round the arcade and it suddenly occurred to Owen that it might provide a vantage point from which he could more pleasantly monitor proceedings.

He climbed up the outside staircase past the fountains surrounded by black-veiled women filling their pots with water and out onto the little parapeted promenade which crowned the second story.

From inside the arcade came the murmur of children's voices. As with many of the larger sebils, the arcaded upper story was occupied by a kuttub, a school where little children received their first lessons on the Koran.

Owen smiled. It was an unexpectedly tender insight on the part of the Arabs to accommodate their infants up here where it was airy and cool.

He walked to the parapet and looked over. Down in the
street he could see some of his men. They approached a house
and went in. Not long afterwards, watching, he saw them
appear on the roof. They looked around for a moment and
then went down.

From where he stood, high up, he could look down on
the roofs of the houses. Most of them were flat and empty,
save for the occasional bundle of firewood, the heap of vegetables,
the pile of cornstalks. One or two of the larger houses, though,
had roof gardens; and, as he watched, two women came up
on to one of these and began watering the plants.

It was a house about two along from the one he had been
looking at previously. He hoped the women would have
completed their task and departed before his men arrived.
Servants would probably warn them but if there was an
outside staircase and his men dashed up—?

He watched anxiously. The men went into the next house
and worked through it. The women went on watering.

The men finished the house and came out into the street.
And at that moment, fortunately, the women left the roof of
their own accord.

Owen breathed a sigh of relief. It wouldn't have done for
the women to be met by his men. That, yet again, could
have caused trouble.

What a country this was to police in! Mosques, bathhouses,
roofs—you could offend someone's susceptibilities by searching any of them. What were you to do? If it wasn't religion,
it was women!

His men, searching both sides of the street, had covered
that block of houses and were now coming up the street towards
the fountain house. He went down to meet them.

"That one next?" said one of the men, indicating the
fountain house with his hand.

"Of course!"

The women watched them curiously as they mounted the stairs. Owen was about to move away when one of his men appeared above the parapet and waved to him urgently.

He ran up.

In an inner room, beyond the chanting class, were some sacks and packaging. The men had picked up the sacks and shaken them out. And out had fallen two new live clips of ammunition.

⟨⟩

"Of course, we're holding the teacher," said Owen.

"That won't do much good," said Garvin scornfully.

"They moved the guns this morning right in front of him."

"This morning?"

Owen swallowed.

"Yes, this morning. When we started searching."

"I thought you had people on the lookout?"

"Well, we did. But—"

"You seem to be mislaying a lot of things lately," said Garvin. "First, the body. Now the guns."

⟨⟩

"He says that all he knows is that the men came this morning and took away the guns," said Nikos, Owen's Official Clerk and Office Manager.

"He must know more than that," protested Owen. "Where the guns were hidden, for a start."

"He says he was told not to use the room."

"Who told him?"

"A man."

"What sort of man?"

"The usual. Galabeah and headdress. The headdress held across his face."

"No description?"

"No description."

"Keep him," said Owen. "It may help him to see better. And send Georgiades down. See if he can find out anything."

But this was bolting the door after the horse had gone. The teacher was unimportant and probably genuinely knew nothing. Georgiades questioned several other people: the kuttub's watchman, a fiki who taught there, people in the neighboring shops, but to no avail. The fact was that the guns had been there and Owen had missed them twice. The first time because he had allowed himself to be called away in the middle of things and hadn't been able to supervise the men properly. The second time because—well, because they had been smart enough to smuggle the guns away right under the noses of the men he had posted to make sure that didn't happen.

He was back where he had started. Only this time without the guns.

⚭

And still there were distractions! Mahmoud had traced the girls who had been on the Prince's dahabeeyah and wanted Owen's help in interviewing them. Owen could guess why that was. They must be foreign.

Because of treaty concessions imposed on Egypt over the centuries, the nationals of certain foreign powers had legal privileges. Their houses could not be entered by the police, for instance; they had to be tried by courts of their own country, not by Egyptian courts, and so on.

The definition of nationality, already elastic in this cosmopolitan country, was easily stretched and all kinds of dubious people claimed benefit of the Capitulations, as the privileges were called.

It was common practice, for example, for a brothel-keeper brought before a court to claim that he or she belonged to a privileged nationality. It was possible, if the police applied to the Consul of a country, to get the exemptions waived. But by the time the police had secured the exemption and got back to the brothel, the keeper would have changed his nationality and they would have to start all over again.

It was another of those things, like religion and women, that required policing to be resourceful in Cairo.

If you were dealing with a foreign national it often paid to have a representative of a Great Power, like Britain, at your back. But it was probably for another reason that Mahmoud had called on him. In a sensitive case like this, where action against foreign nationals might have diplomatic repercussions, it was wise to get the British on your side first.

Owen knew this and didn't mind it. There were even advantages in that he might be able to "manage" the affair better from the inside. All the same, just now it was a distraction.

However, he went. The two girls, it transpired, did not work in a cabaret but assisted at a gambling salon. Owen thought he knew what kind of assistance that was but Mahmoud said it was not like that, or not like that entirely.

"It's a very high-class salon," he said, "and the people who go there are more interested in gambling. They tend to be European, though, or Europeanized Egyptians and expect the social style of a club on the Riviera. There's a reception area where they can sit and talk and the girls sit in there too and help the conversation along."

At the request of the salon's owner they met the girls not at the salon but in a hotel nearby. The salon was in the Ismailia quarter where all the best hotels were. They met in the Hotel Continental.

When they arrived they were taken at once to a private alcove. Owen was amused to see that hospitality had been provided. That wouldn't get far with Mahmoud, who, strict Muslim that he was, drank only coffee.

The women must already have been there, for the maître d'hôtel brought them immediately. They were dressed in discreet though well-cut black and, in deference to the customs of the country, long veils, which they put aside as soon as they sat down. One was Belgian, the other Hungarian. Their names were Nanette and Masha.

"We've got other names, too," they pointed out. Mahmoud addressed them as Mademoiselle.

Yes, they had been on the dahabeeyah. They had been approached beforehand and had agreed to go to Luxor and back as members of the Prince's party.

"A Prince, after all," said Nanette, with a roll of her eyes.

Masha was less impressed. Apparently, princes were two a penny in Hungary.

"What did that entail?" asked Owen.

"What do you mean?"

"How friendly did you have to be?"

Nanette shrugged her shoulders.

"So-so," she said.

They had met Narouz previously.

"He came to the salon. Not regularly. He would come several times in a week and then you wouldn't see him for ages."

He liked talking to them, they said. Just talking. They wouldn't have minded other things too but talking was what he wanted.

"He could get as much of the other as he liked," said Masha. "The one thing he couldn't get in Egypt, he said, was intelligent female conversation. It's the lives they lead," she explained. "Shut up in those harems!"

"You're not saying he came to the salon just for conversation?"

"No, no. He liked gambling. But when he wasn't playing he liked to talk."

"Especially with women," said Nanette.

"And it was as a result of these conversations that he invited you to join him on the dahabeeyah?"

"Yes. He said it was the only thing that would get him through it."

"I don't understand," said Mahmoud. "Are you saying he didn't want to go up to Luxor?"

"He hated going on the river at all. He said it was slow and boring."

"Then why—"

Nanette shrugged. "He said he was doing it only because it was his duty."

"Duty? I don't understand that."

Nanette shrugged again.

The two girls had been fetched by car, the Prince's car, from the salon and been taken to the river at Beni Suef, where the dahabeeyah had called in for them.

What about the other girl?

A little silence.

"We didn't know her," said Nanette.

"She wasn't one of us," said Masha.

"Meaning?"

"She was Egyptian for a start," said Masha.

"What kind of Egyptian? Levantine Egyptian, Greek Egyptian, Italian Egyptian—?"

"Egyptian Egyptian."

"Are you sure?"

"Yes. She told us about her family once. Her father's a big merchant or something. They have a big house. Only she doesn't live there anymore."

"Didn't," said Masha.

Nanette shrugged again: a sudden, nervous jerk.

"Where has she been living up to now?" asked Mahmoud.

"With an aunt, I think."

"Do you know where?"

"No."

"We'd never seen her before," said Masha, "not till we got into the car."

"She was already in the car? He'd picked her up first?"

"I suppose so."

The girl hadn't said much, then or at any other time. She had kept herself to herself. Owen had the impression that this was the first time for her, as it certainly wasn't for the other two. From what they said, she had shrunk into a shell from the moment she had got on board, going off by herself whenever she could.

"And that was why she was on the upper deck that night?" asked Owen.

"Yes. She was always up there."

Mahmoud got them to go through the events of the night. The women had got into the way of going up on the deck every evening. They liked it even if Narouz didn't. They had sensed the disapproval of the Rais.

"But what's the point of going up to Luxor if you never get a chance to see anything?" asked Nanette.

What indeed?

"Besides, after being cooped up below decks all day—"

She made a pretty *moue*, which, Owen decided, was probably intended for his benefit.

"You were up there together," said Mahmoud, unsoftened, "all three?"

"Yes."

"What were you talking about?"

"What were we talking about? I can't remember." The girls looked at each other. "This and that."

"Did she join in?"

"A little. Not much."

They had grown so used to her not joining in that they had not really noticed that she had stayed up there when they came down.

"We were hoping we might have a drink before dinner," said Masha.

"Some hope!" said Nanette.

It was when they were assembling for dinner that they had noticed her absence. They had called up to her. Narouz had even gone up.

"Why he bothered I can't think," said Nanette tartly.

They had started the first course without her. Then, as she still failed to appear, Narouz became annoyed and sent the eunuch up to fetch her.

"We thought at first that she had hidden herself deliberately," said Nanette, "and didn't bother too much. But then as time went by—"

It all corroborated what they had already heard. Mahmoud probed but came up with nothing more.

"You know where to find us," said Nanette, getting up.

"Any evening," said Masha, "except Friday."

Owen put out his hand to stop them.

"Just one other thing," he said, "before you go. What was her name?"

"Leila," said Nanette. "That was it, wasn't it? Leila."

☙⟐❧

"Well," said the Prince, "how are you getting on?"

"Fine. But there are just one or two things I would like to ask you," said Mahmoud.

"Naturally," said the Prince, settling back upon the divan. Owen had wondered whether his rooms would be furnished Eastern style or Western style. There was, however, no equivalent of the green motorcar. The room was like any other in the wealthier Cairo houses: carpets on the wall, tiles on the floor, low divans, cushions and very little furniture of any other sort.

"Could you tell me first," said Mahmoud, "why you were making an expedition to Luxor?"

"I was *not* making an expedition to Luxor. That makes me sound like your English tomb-robbers. I was merely making a boring journey by river and Luxor happened to be at the end of it."

"What, then, was the purpose of your boring journey?"

The Prince, unexpectedly, was silent for a moment.

"I was accompanying my nephew," he said then.

"The Prince Fahid?"

"Exactly."

"And what was the purpose of Prince Fahid's journey?"

"To add to his knowledge. He is reaching the age, you see, when he will be expected to play a larger part in public affairs. So we are trying to introduce him to the larger world. He has not even seen yet all the Khedivial estates. There is one not far from Luxor. That is what we went to see."

"You did not stay there very long."

"Quite long enough. Once seen, better quickly forgotten. I believe my father hoped we would stay longer. But Fahid is, like myself, someone on whom the attractions of the desert quickly pall."

"Would it be possible for us to talk to the Prince?"

"I thought you might like to see him." Narouz clapped his hands. A servant came in. "Ask the Prince Fahid to come this way, will you? This, too," he said confidingly to Mahmoud and Owen, "will add to his experience."

A young boy came into the room. He looked inquiringly at Narouz and then came across to the two men, bowed and shook hands.

"More familiar," said Narouz, slightly crossly. "And Captain Owen is British. Just shake hands."

The boy was not in the least off-put. He just stood there smiling easily.

He was, Owen judged, about fourteen, a little below medium height and slim, although already showing signs of broadening out like his uncle. His face was delicate, almost girlish, with long eyelashes and large brown eyes.

He answered Mahmoud's questions readily enough. They had been to the estate, yes. No, they hadn't stayed long—a little amused glance at Narouz here. The journey had been interesting, yes. Quite, that was. He would have preferred a motorboat. His uncle was going to take him on one when they next went to Cannes.

Luxor? Like most Egyptians, he took the past for granted and was not particularly interested in it. The river? Was merely the river. The landscape, familiar since childhood, was not worthy of remark. There was something practical, matter-of-fact about the boy. If the dahabeeyah had had an engine room Owen could have imagined him poking around happily in it. He was not one for admiring the sunset.

The night the girl had disappeared; he remembered it well. A serious look came over his face. They had been about to have dinner. It was an important occasion because his uncle was to have initiated him into the mysteries of handling langoustines. When the girl hadn't come down, his uncle had been angry and sent the eunuch up. They had started without her. And then, of course, the eunuch had returned.

"You see," said Narouz, after Fahid had shaken hands all round and departed, "he's very inexperienced. They spend too long in the harem these days."

"He's surely not still—"

"Of course not. He's been out for some time. He has private tutors. English, French and Italian. But I sometimes think they are just as bad."

The harem. Would it be possible to speak with the ladies of the harem, Mahmoud asked diffidently. They had after all been on board.

The Prince's face clouded over.

"I don't know about that," he said doubtfully. Then his face cleared. "Why not?" he said enthusiastically. "It will be something different for them."

He summoned the ladies of the harem. They appeared, wrapped like their less exalted sisters from head to foot in black, and ostensibly reluctant. Over their veils, though, their eyes sparkled.

They answered Mahmoud's questions demurely and vacuously.

"Oh, come on!" said the Prince crossly, getting bored. "Speak up!"

They had been having dinner separately in the harem quarters, as they always did, the night that it happened. No,

they hadn't been aware of anything untoward, not until, much
later, the eunuch had come down and searched below deck
inch by inch from bows to stern. That had been rather exciting
and they were prepared to recount it at considerable length
until Narouz intervened and told them to shut up.

Mahmoud asked them about the girl. The sparkle went
out of their eyes, the veils, which had been slipping, came
up. They had, alas, hardly spoken to her.

"Which is not surprising," said Narouz, returning after
chivvying them out. "It would hardly be proper for them to
speak to such women. Though it might give them ideas," he
added wistfully.

"Would that also be true of Leila?" asked Mahmoud.

The Prince looked at him quickly.

"Why do you ask?"

"You said 'such women,' I wondered if Leila was the same
sort of women as the other two."

"They were foreign, of course."

"Yes, and that puzzles me. I can see how they came to be
with you. But Leila was not foreign and it is unusual for one
of our women to do things like that. I wondered how it came
about?"

"It is unusual, yes, but not so out of the common. Especially if the Khedive wishes."

"Did the Khedive wish?"

"I was thinking of myself."

"But for you to wish, you must have already known her.
How did you come across her in the first place?"

"In the first place? I hardly remember."

"In the second place, then," said Mahmoud quietly, recog-
nizing that he was being fenced with. "For you certainly knew
her."

Again the sharp glance from the Prince.

"She had been about the Court."

"Come!" said Mahmoud, a trifle wearily. "About the Court?"

"Not in the strict sense, of course. My father doesn't have that sort of thing. Not in public."

"You met her at the Palace?"

"Not exactly at the Palace."

"Where, then?"

"About."

"These things are important, Prince."

"Why are they important?"

"We need to know her identity."

The Prince rubbed his chin. "Yes," he said. "Yes. I thought you would."

"Well, then?"

"This is the embarrassing part. I don't know."

"Come!"

"I know you don't believe me but it's true. I don't even know her name. Well, no, that's not true. Her name was Leila. But that is all I know. I do not know her family."

"Are you sure, Prince?"

"She did not wish me to know her family. I used to tease her about it. 'Little Miss No-Name from Nowhere.' She would not say. She was, I think," said the Prince, "ashamed."

"Where did you meet her?"

"At a play. I do not ordinarily go to Egyptian plays. I find them unredeemingly turgid. This one, I was assured, was different. It was by a modern playwright. I went in the belief that I was encouraging a modern renaissance of the Egyptian theater. I was," said the Prince, "horribly mistaken. The play was as turgid as ever. And, what was worse, ridiculously radical."

"The girl?"

"I met her afterwards, backstage. There was a party. Naturally I had been invited. Foolishly I went, to encourage, as I say, the theater. It was awful. The one interesting thing was the girl. I met her again afterwards. Several times. And then I thought of inviting her to accompany me on this foolish expedition."

"Could you tell me the name of the play?"

"*New Roses in the Garden.*" The Prince shuddered. "Never again. The avant-garde is not for me. Not in the theater anyway."

He looked at his watch.

"Perhaps we can continue some other time," said Mahmoud, rising dutifully.

"Of course. Of course."

He accompanied them to the door. At the door he hesitated.

"You have not," he said diffidently, "not yet found the body?"

"I am afraid not."

"No? Well, I expect you will."

He hesitated again and then suddenly brightened.

"Of course," he said, "if you don't...Well, there ceases to be a problem, doesn't there? No body, no crime."

Chapter 4

"No problem?" said Zeinab, outraged. "The girl is dead, isn't she?"

"We can't be sure of that," said Owen cautiously.

"No? You think she jumped off the top of that boat and swam to the shore?"

"Well, in principle she could have done—"

"Egyptian girls," said Zeinab haughtily, "do not swim."

Owen was beginning to wish he hadn't told her.

"In any case," he said, "Narouz is wrong. Just because there isn't a body, that doesn't mean there couldn't be a case. A potential crime has been reported. The report itself is sufficient to trigger things. An investigation has been started and it will continue until, well, the file is closed. It has become a bureaucratic matter now."

"There are times," said Zeinab, "when you sound boringly cold-blooded."

"The investigation will continue," Owen contented himself with saying.

"Oh, good." Zeinab brooded awhile. Then she said, "It will continue, yes, but will it get anywhere?"

"We've only just started," said Owen defensively.

"You haven't got very far yet," Zeinab pointed out.

"It's a difficult case."

"That is because you started in the wrong place. With the body, not with Leila."

"We don't know anything about Leila yet."

"That's just what I'm saying. You ought to find out about her. What sort of girl she was, how she came to do something like this—"

"Something like *what?*" asked Owen, exasperated. "It's not what she's done, it's what's been done to her."

"How did she come to be on the dahabeeyah?" demanded Zeinab. "That's not a thing a normal Egyptian girl would have done. Even I wouldn't have done a thing like that!"

"We'll try to find out. We *are* trying to find out. Only—"

"What was the name of that play?" demanded Zeinab, disregarding his patter. "The one Narouz met her at?"

"*New Roses in the Garden*. Pretty dreadful, too, according to Narouz."

"But I know that play," said Zeinab. "It's Gamal's latest. We received an invitation."

"Did we?"

"Yes. You didn't go."

Owen enjoyed Zeinab's artistic friends. And he liked Gamal, whose acquaintance he had first made when working on one of his earliest cases as Mamur Zapt. At the time Gamal had written a number of plays but none of them had yet actually been produced. Since then several had reached the boards. The audiences, though, had been confined to the especially perceptive.

"It would have been the opening night," said Zeinab. "I couldn't go, so I went to the second night. You couldn't go either. You were down in Minya Province running after that Gypsy girl."

"No I wasn't!"

This was an old charge. Quite unjustified.

"While I was left in Cairo. Alone," said Zeinab, unforgiving.

"This is beside the point."

"No it isn't. Because if you had not been down in Minya chasing that Gypsy woman you would have been at the theater. And then you would have met Leila. So," said Zeinab, "it's all your fault."

Owen was silenced for a moment. Then he recovered.

"So it is. You're right. If I had not been chasing that Gypsy woman I could have gone to the party and chased Leila."

"You will not deflect me," said Zeinab, "with your perverse remarks. I intend to find out whether she was there that night and who Leila was."

⟨⟩

Mahmoud, adopting more orthodox procedures, was also trying to establish Leila's identity.

"So," he was saying to the Prince's chauffeur as Owen arrived, "you picked the two girls up from the salon and took them to the river at Beni Suef?"

"If that's what they say, yes."

"It's not what they say, it's what you say," said Mahmoud sternly.

The man shrugged, confident in the power of the Prince to protect, at least against the Parquet. A confidence which Mahmoud had anticipated and which he had invited Owen along to undermine.

"This is the Mamur Zapt," he said. "Be careful how you answer."

The man flinched slightly.

"I shall answer as I please," he said, but less boldly. Something of the Mamur Zapt's old aura still clung to the post. To it was added a certain unpredictability these days because of its British incumbency.

"You picked the two girls up?" Mahmoud repeated.

"Yes."

"That is better. And now you are speaking with your own voice. Let us keep it that way. You took them to the river at Beni Suef?"

"Yes."

"Good. And there you waited till the dahabeeyah came in. At which point you put the women on board. Yes?"

"Yes."

"But," pursued Mahmoud, "there were three women, were there not?"

"If you say so."

"I would like to hear you say so. With your own voice."

"Three women, then," said the chauffeur.

"So where did this other woman come from?"

The man hesitated.

"Tell us the truth," said Owen, speaking for the first time. "And remember that we may already know it. Remember, too, that we do not have to ask you here. I may take you back to the Bab el Khalk and ask you."

"I picked her up too," said the chauffeur.

"Of course. And where did you pick her up? Not from the salon, was it?"

"No. I had picked her up first, before going to the salon. She was waiting for me."

"And waiting for you where?"

"I was to pick her up by the Souk Al-Gadira."

"*By* the Souk Al-Gadira? Did you not pick her up from a house?"

"No, effendi"—the chauffeur was being polite now—"the souk there is where four roads meet. The streets are narrow and twist and turn and it is not advisable to take a car up them. Not a car like this one."

There was a note of reverence in the chauffeur's voice. All the time he talked he kept his hand on the bonnet, partly for reassurance—he was less confident than he seemed—and partly as a caress.

"So where did you meet?"

"At the junction of the Sharia el Garb with the Sharia el Hakim. I was told she would be waiting for me."

"Who told you?"

The chauffeur looked very unhappy.

"Effendi," he whispered, "I—I do not think I should say." The Prince, then.

"Had you been to the spot before?"

Eventually they brought him to admit that he had either collected the girl from or returned the girl to the spot on several occasions over the last two months.

"And did you ever go with the girl to her house? Think before you speak."

Never. The chauffeur swore on the Book. He had always delivered her to the same spot. Always. He had stayed in the car. She had never asked him to accompany her home. He would have been reluctant to accede if she had. Who knew what might befall the car if left unattended? "Effendi," said the chauffeur earnestly, "there are bad men abroad." Worst; there were small boys. It was clear that, for the chauffeur at least, cars had priority over women.

The chauffeur, then, had no idea where the girl lived? He had not. He was prepared to swear it on the Book.

Nevertheless, Owen thought he might be speaking the truth.

Mahmoud tried one last way. Had the chauffeur ever picked up the Prince from the neighborhood? Or delivered him to a house in that vicinity? He stopped the chauffeur wearily before he got to the Book.

☙

Owen went down to the souk himself. The man he was looking for, a Greek, was sitting at a table outside a café, deep in conversation with three Arabs. From time to time, almost absentmindedly, he reached into his pocket and produced a sweet, which he gave to any small boy who happened to be near. There were, naturally, quite a lot of small boys near.

The Greek was deep in a dramatic tale of misadventure.

"And then, by God, it pulled out to miss a donkey and I looked, lo, and it was coming straight towards me! I threw myself against the wall and prayed. And God must have heard my prayers, for it passed by me leaving me unharmed."

"God is great!" said the rapt audience.

"Unharmed," said the Greek, "but not untouched. For as it passed, it reached out and caught my sleeve and rent it. And I stumbled and would have fallen had it not been for the wall."

"God is indeed merciful!"

"He is indeed!" agreed the Greek.

"Such things ought not to be," said one of his hearers.

"That is true. And do you know what I believe to be at the root of the problem?"

His listeners shook their heads.

"Speed," declared the Greek. "That's what it is. People are trying to go too fast."

"True. Oh, very true."

"It is the curse of the age."

"What is wrong with donkeys?" asked one of the men.

"That's what I say. God put man in the world. He put donkeys in the world. But he did not put cars!"

"That is true," said his hearers, impressed. They volunteered their own embroiderings of the theme.

The Greek could not, however, put the incident out of his mind.

"It was a mighty car," he said, "and painted green."

"Green?" said one of the small boys, all of whom had been following the conversation as closely as the men.

"Yes. And that is not right, either. For green is the color of the Prophet and—"

The small boy, however, was not interested.

"I have seen a green car," he said. "It comes down here."

"What sort of car?"

The boy described it.

"The very car!" declared the Greek. He slipped the boy two large boiled sweets and turned to his friends across the table.

"Be warned!" he said. "Lest you, too, be crushed and defiled! Guard your footsteps! Look over your shoulder!"

Etcetera, etcetera. His hearers enjoyed every minute of it. Cairenes liked a good alarm.

The Greek, satisfied with the effect of his story, rose from his seat, shook hands all round and prepared to depart. At the last moment he caught sight of Owen, who had taken up position at an adjoining table, and raised hands to heaven.

"My friend!" he declared. "And I had not seen you!"

Owen rose to greet him and they embraced like long-lost brothers. The Greek was persuaded—needed no persuasion, really—to sit down. More coffee was called for. The Greek's friends at his previous table watched benignly; and the phalanx of small boys switched support.

The Greek continued to feed them with sweets. And then, after he and Owen had been talking for some while, he crooked his finger and called over the boy who had seen the car.

"My friend has in interest in our car," he said. The small boy swelled with the pride of implied shared possession.

"It is a good car," he said.

"Sadly, though—and this is the way of the world as you will find out when you grow up—my friend is less interested in the car itself than in some of the people it carries. One in particular." He winked at the boy. "Did not the car, when it stopped here, pick up a fine young woman?"

"I don't know about fine," said the boy. "It picked up Leila."

"There!" said the Greek to Owen. "I knew it! And he even knows her name!"

"Leila Sekhmet," said the boy.

"And she lives near here?"

"Just up the street."

"Show me the house," said the Greek, "and if it should happen that on the way we meet a sweet-seller…"

It did so happen. The Greek purchased a bag of sweets, well, not so much a bag as a twist of newspaper, distributed some of the sweets among his retinue of small boys and gave the rest to his guide.

"It may be that future conversation could benefit us both," he said.

The boy led them up one of the dark streets to a place where the houses were tall and thin and so closely packed together that door followed immediately upon door. He stopped outside one of these.

"Leila lives here?"

"Yes."

"Who does the house belong to?"

"Mrs. Rabaq."

"And who is Mrs. Rabaq?"

"Leila's aunt."

The Greek knocked on the door. After some moments it was opened by an elderly woman servant.

"Please announce me to Mrs. Rabaq," said the Greek. "Tell her we come about Leila."

The woman stood still.

"Who are you?" she said.

"This is the Mamur Zapt," said the Greek, indicating Owen.

The woman's eyes swept over him.

"I shall not tell her that," she said.

She stumped away. They heard her steps going up the stairs. It was a while before they returned.

"She will see you." The woman hesitated. "She is very old," she said, "and no longer understands things clearly. But she will see you."

The room was closely shuttered and very dark. The only light was from a dim kerosene lamp standing on a low table. There was a sofa in the middle of the room on which an old woman was sitting. She had pulled her veil right over her face so that they could not even see her eyes.

"Leila is my niece," she said. "What has happened to her?"

She had spoken in Arabic and Owen replied in Arabic. He fell naturally into the courteous, familiar mode used to address the elderly.

"We do not know that anything has happened to her, mother," he said. "But we fear."

"I fear too," said the woman. "I always fear."

"We fear that an accident may have befallen her."

The woman drew her breath in sharply. Then she stood up.

"I will go to her. Tell me where she is. I will go—"

She swayed and put out her hand. Owen caught her and eased her gently back on to the sofa.

"When the time comes, mother," he said soothingly. "If it comes. But it has not come yet. At the moment it is just that she is missing."

"She is always missing," said the old woman querulously. "It is not right. She comes and goes as she pleases. My sister's daughter. We were never like that. Our father would never have allowed—"

She put her hand to her head.

"Leila!" she said and burst into tears.

The servant, who had followed them into the room, put her arms round her and comforted her.

"It is time you went to bed," she said.

She helped the old woman up and led her across the room. At the door the old woman shook herself free.

"Wait!" she said. "Who are these men, Khadija? Why are they here?"

"It is nothing, mother," said the servant. "Come!"

She led her out through the door. "Do not go," she said over her shoulder to Owen and the Greek. "I will come down shortly."

They waited quietly. The furniture was old, the furnishings sparse.

They heard the servant returning. She went on past the door of the room. When she came back it was with a tray, coffee cups and sugar.

"Be seated."

She came back again, this time with a brazier and coffee-pot. She stirred the ashes and placed the coffeepot in the middle.

"That is proper," she said with satisfaction. "That is the way it used to be."

She poured them some coffee.

"So," she said to Owen, "you're the Mamur Zapt, are you?"

"That is so, mother."

He addressed her in the same way as he had her mistress, with the deference due to age.

"What has she done wrong?"

"Leila? I do not know that she has done anything wrong. Except, perhaps, that she has stayed out too late at night."

"She has certainly done that. But does the Mamur Zapt interest himself in things like that?"

"I think she is dead. And the Mamur Zapt *does* interest himself in things like that."

The woman had not bothered to pull her veil across her face. She stared at Owen with large, unblinking eyes.

"How did she die?"

"I think she may have drowned."

"Drowned? How could she have drowned?"

"She was on the river. In a dahabeeyah."

"I do not understand. How could she have been on the river? In a dahabeeyah?"

"Did you know nothing of it?"

"Nothing."

"Nor who she was with?"

The woman gave a little hard laugh.

"It is that, is it? No," she said, "no. No, she never told me. And I thought it best not to ask."

"You did not approve?"

"How could I? It was wrong to leave her family in the first place, wrong, having come here, to go on leading the life she did."

"What sort of life was that?"

"When she was a child she was a pretty little thing. Her father doted on her. We all did. I, her mother. The only child, although a girl child. Her father took her with us when we went to France. And that was a big mistake, for there she saw and was seen."

Among the men she was seen by was a young man from another rich Alexandrian family and when they all returned to Egypt he somehow succeeded in gaining access to her.

"He said to her: 'Let us be free, as the young in France are free.' And she was thrilled by that, for she found it hard to come back to a woman's life in Egypt after tasting life in France. Before, she knew no better. Now, she wanted holiday all the time."

The young man's intentions had been honorable and he had asked his father to obtain her as a bride. His father, however, had had other ideas. Perhaps Leila's family had not been quite good enough for him. Perhaps it was just that he had already made other plans. Marriages in middle-class Egyptian families were made by the father, usually without reference to the son or daughter, and sometimes without even reference to the mother. Anyway, the boy's father had refused.

Leila's father had somehow got to hear of it and in her case, of course, the consequences were worse. Her father, lax before, now kept her immured. She was not even allowed to receive female visitors.

Leila had both pined and rebelled. Somehow she again made contact with the young man. And one night they had eloped.

"What happened next I do not know," said the servant, "but a year later she came to our house here and threw herself into the mistress's arms and begged her to take her in. Of course she said yes. Leila was her sister's child. Besides, she had none of her own and Leila had always been a favorite. And I thought at first that it was good, because my mistress had lost her interest in life and I thought this might renew it."

She lifted the pot, stirred the ashes and then replaced it. The action seemed to break her train of thought, for afterwards she did not resume speaking, seemed to forget she had been speaking and sat waiting passively. Owen realized suddenly that like her mistress she was old.

"You thought that at first," he prompted gently, "but afterwards you changed your mind?"

She came back with a start.

"Not at first. She was so glad to be with us and we were so glad to have her. The mistress fussed over her—still does—and they were like mother and daughter. And Leila needed a mother. But then—" She broke off.

"Then?" Owen prompted softly.

"The mistress became—as she is now. Leila nursed her tenderly. But as the months went by she became restless. She was a young woman now and needed more. She needed a man. She started to go out."

"She had friends?"

"Yes. Some she had met—when she was with him. I do not know what sort of friends they were that they would let a young woman come to them on her own! But soon she was always with them."

"Nights?"

"No," said the woman. "Well, once or twice, perhaps. She said she had been to the theater and that afterwards they had talked late. I did not press. I did not want to know. The theater!" She shuddered. "What sort of place is that for a woman to go to? If that was the sort of friends they were—!"

"Did she tell you any of their names?"

"No."

Owen thought.

"I would like to see her room. Perhaps she kept names, addresses."

The woman hesitated uncertainly.

"Are you married?" she asked suddenly.

"Me? No."

"It would not be proper."

"How about him?" said Owen, indicating the Greek. "He is married."

The woman surveyed the Greek closely.

"Yes," she said, "I can see that. How many wives have you got?" she asked with interest.

"One," said the Greek. "That is more than enough."

The woman cackled.

"She keeps you on a tight rein, does she? That is proper," she said approvingly. "Very well," she said, "I will show you her room."

Owen, alone in the room, poured himself some more coffee. There was an old shiraz carpet on the wall, very faded, an old, full-length incredibly elaborate mirror, some old pots, Persian boxes. No money in the house now, he thought, but money in the past. He wondered about Leila's family.

Georgiades came back shaking his head. Owen stood up.

"Thank you," he said to the old servant woman. "You have been very helpful. There is just one thing more: I feel I should tell Leila's parents. Can you give me their names and tell me where I might find them?"

The woman stood very still.

"She is dead to them already," she said bitterly. "Why do you bring a dead body back from the grave?"

⊙∞∞9

Since he was in the area, Owen decided he would go down to the river and take another look at the shoal on which Leila's body had come to rest. His way took him past the local police station. Sitting on the ground in front of it were the two constables who had delayed him at the dovecot during the arms search. They greeted him cheerfully.

"Hello," they said. "Any nearer finding that body?"

"Yes," said Owen. "I'm nearer."

"Good. Tell us when you find it."

"Don't worry," said Owen. "I will."

He would too, he promised himself. He was sure they knew something, some trick that that idle, rascally District Chief had been up to. There had been something they'd said. What was it?

And then he stopped in his tracks, turned and made his way in a quite different direction.

He found the watchman asleep under a tree, his legs curled up under him as they had been when he had pantomimed the way he had found the body, his turban neatly parked beside him. Owen stirred him gently with his foot.

The man's eyes opened.

"Effendi!" he said in alarm, scrambling to his feet.

"I am sorry to disturb you, Abu," said Owen, "but there are things I would know."

"I will help you if I can," the man said doubtfully, "but I have told you all I know."

"Not quite all. Let us go back to the moment you found the body, the moment you realized that it *was* a body. What did you do?"

"I went to the Chief to report it."

"This was at the police station, was it?"

"Yes, effendi."

"Was he alone?"

"No, effendi. Fazal was with him. Fazal had just come in and they were talking. They were talking"—Abu lowered his eyes bashfully—"about you, effendi."

"About me?"

"Yes, effendi. Fazal said that you had met up with the men and had started work. And the Chief said: 'Already? Before God, they must have little work to do.' That is what he said, effendi."

"Did he?" said Owen grimly.

"It is all the same with these great people—this is what he said, effendi. They have nothing better to do than go down

and make a nuisance of themselves to people who are peacefully going about their own affairs. That is what he said."

"Really?"

"Yes. And then he turned on me and shouted: 'And here
is another! What have you brought me to spoil my day, Abu?'
And I told him, and he said: 'What do I care about bodies?
Let it lie there.' And Fazal said: 'You had better not do that if
the Mamur Zapt is about.' And the Chief said, 'That is true,
Fazal.' And he thought, and then he said: 'I know what we
will do, Fazal. You go and tell the Mamur Zapt that there is
urgent business at the river. Let him see to it.' And then he
laughed and said: 'This is the way to do it, Fazal. Let us get
the great working for us for a change.'"

"Thank you," said Owen. "Very interesting."

"That was good, wasn't it, effendi?" said Abu happily. "To
have you working for him and not the other way round."

"Oh, very good. So Fazal went off to fetch me. And then
what?"

"Then the Chief picked up the phone and said to me:
'And while we are at it, let us get those other idle bastards off
their backsides.' Pardon, effendi, that is what he said."

"Go on. Who did he phone?"

"The Parquet, I think. And one other. And then he said
to me: 'Push off, Abu! Get back to the river lest the Mamur
Zapt come and find no one there.' So I went."

"What about Ibrahim? Was he sent with you?"

"Yes, effendi. The Chief put his head out of the office and
called for him and said: 'Go with Abu. There is a body. You
know what to do.' 'Yes,' said Ibrahim, 'I know what to do.'
And so we went together."

"That," said Owen, "is most interesting."

"Is it, effendi?" said Abu, greatly gratified.

"Yes. But still puzzling. Tell me, Abu: you went to the
river together?"

"Yes, effendi."

"That is what I find puzzling. Are you sure?"

"Yes, effendi."

"All the way? Together?"

"Yes, effendi. Well, Ibrahim asked me to call in at Mohammed Fingari's to get a package for him. And that was strange because Mohammed said, 'What package is this?' And I said—"

"OK, OK," said Owen. "I get the idea. You went in to get the package while Ibrahim went on to the river—was that it?"

"Yes, effendi."

"So you joined him there?"

"Yes, effendi. And he chided me, saying: 'Where have you been, Abu? What if the Mamur Zapt had come in your absence?' And I said: 'It is not my fault, Ibrahim. You—'"

"Thank you. Thank you. I understand. So in fact Ibrahim arrived at the river first?"

"Yes, effendi."

"Alone?"

"Yes, effendi. Until I got there. Which wasn't long, effendi, really. I swear it. It was just that—"

"Thank you. You have told me what I wished to know."

"I have?"

"Yes. And now we will go to the Chief."

Abu fell in beside him. He was clearly, however, turning things over in his mind.

"Effendi," he said diffidently.

"Yes?"

"If I have said anything untoward, the Chief will bear me."

"If what you have told me is true, it will be the Chief who is beaten."

෴

"So tell me, Ibrahim, what happened when you and Abu went down to the river?"

The constable scratched his head.

"What happened? Nothing happened. When we got there, the body wasn't there. If it ever had been there."

"You went to the river together?"

"Indeed."

"All the way—together?"

"Yes. More or less."

"You did not go on ahead?"

"No, effendi. Well, if I did, that was because Abu took so long. Yes, I remember, effendi." He turned to Owen, "I waited, but that foolish fellow took so long—having a cup of tea, no doubt—that I was worried lest you come and find the corpse unattended, so I hurried on."

"Alone?"

"Well, yes, alone."

"And what did you do when you came to the river?"

"To the river? Nothing. I waited for Abu. It was but a minute, effendi. And then you came."

"You weren't there long?"

"No, effendi."

"But long enough to fetch the pole?"

Ibrahim's jaw dropped.

"Pole?" he said.

"That's what you use, isn't it? To push the bodies off? So that they float down to the next district and you don't have to report them?"

The Chief had gone pale.

"That is correct, isn't it?" Owen addressed him. "That is the usual practice, is it not?"

The Chief found it hard to speak.

"Sometimes," he said at last.

"Only this time it was a mistake. For you had already summoned me. And notified the Parquet. You did not mean it to happen this time. Only Ibrahim misunderstood you. 'You know what to do,' you said to him. And he thought he knew what that meant."

The corporal shot the Chief an agonized glance.

"So he got rid of Abu and hurried on ahead. And when he got to the river he took the pole—and he pushed the body off!"

"Effendi—"

"That is what happened, didn't it?"

"Effendi—"

"This time," said Owen, "you had better speak the truth."

"Effendi," said Ibrahim desperately, "that is what would have happened if—"

"Yes?"

"If the body had been there!"

Chapter 5

"What?"

Mahmoud sprang out of his chair.

"Sit down, sit down," said Owen hurriedly, looking around him at the crowded café. The clientele, however, used to the drama of Arab conversation, went on placidly reading their newspapers.

"What did you say?"

"They pushed them off. So that they floated down to the next district and they wouldn't have to bother."

"Pushed them off?"

Mahmoud could hardly believe his ears, refused to believe his ears.

"Yes. There was a special pole they used. That was what gave me the clue. The constables mentioned a pole."

"But this, this is—"

Mahmoud, incoherent with fury, could not for the moment say what it was.

"Outrageous!" he shouted.

"Yes, yes. Come on, sit down," said Owen, plucking at his arm. Mahmoud shook him off.

"Disgraceful!"

"Yes, yes. I know. Come on—"

"I'll have their blood!" stormed Mahmoud. "I'll have their blood for this!"

He smashed his fist down on the table.

This did attract the attention of some of the newspaper readers. It even attracted the attention of the waiter, which was much more difficult. He came across and dabbed up the spilled coffee with a dirty dishcloth and a flourish.

"By all means," said Owen soothingly. "Have their blood. But have some coffee first."

He coaxed Mahmoud back into his chair.

"It is tampering with the evidence!" shouted Mahmoud.

"Yes, yes."

"Evidence is what the whole system is based on. If we cannot trust that, where are we?"

"Fortunately we found out."

"Yes."

Mahmoud quieted down and raised a fresh cup of coffee to his lips. Suddenly he crashed it down again.

"In this one case!" he shouted. He sprang to his feet. "What about the others? The ones we have not found out? You said there were others. The pole! There was a special pole they used for the purpose. That was what you said. There must be others!"

"The bodies will have turned up lower down. Come on, sit down. They'll have been reported, they'll be in the system. All we have to do is to check back. Sit down!"

Mahmoud reluctantly allowed himself to be pulled down.

"It's the principle of the thing," he said to Owen. "It's the principle."

For Mahmoud it was. He had a vision of the legal system as the expression of a clear, abstract principle of justice and believed that practice should correspond. Unfortunately, this being Egypt, the relation of the operating parts of the system to the ideal vision was somewhat cloudy. This was a perpetual source of vexation to Mahmoud and his efforts to do something about it drove him towards reform at the political level—he was a member of the Nationalist party—and perfectionism in his daily work.

He identified so strongly with the system at its most ideal that when practice fell short, as it invariably did, he took it personally. When the servants of justice revealed shortcomings, as in this case of the local Chief and his constable, he felt it almost as personal betrayal.

"This kind of thing makes a mockery of the whole system," he said bitterly.

"It's just a pair of lazy sods," said Owen.

"To you, perhaps. To me, they are part of the system. And when part of the system fails, the system as a whole fails."

He brooded over his coffee.

"It doesn't matter to you much, does it?" he suddenly shot at Owen.

"Not much," Owen admitted.

"Why is that? Is it because you don't expect any better of Egyptians anyway?"

"No."

The conversation had suddenly moved, as conversation between British and Egyptians often did, into a minefield.

"No," Owen said carefully, very carefully. "It's just that I don't think in terms of system as much as you do."

Mahmoud looked at him intently and then suddenly relaxed.

"I know what it is," he said, smiling. "It is that you are British. No,"—he quickly laid his hand on Owen's arm in the Arab way—"I did not mean it like that. I meant that you British are always pragmatic. Whereas I"—he sighed theatrically and smote himself on the chest—"am Arab."

"French."

Mahmoud looked startled. "French?" he said.

"In this case. The emphasis on system is French, not Arab. You are a true Parquet lawyer, my friend."

"Not Arab? Ah well, it is very confusing being an Egyptian."

They both laughed and then sat sipping their coffee equably. Owen had, however, the sense of relief that follows a near miss.

It was often like that in conversation with educated Egyptians. Partly it was normal Arab volatility, their ability to move from elation to depression, rage to calm, in the space of a few bewildering seconds. Partly, though, it was the explosive potential inherent in any true conversation between a representative of a dominating power and one of the dominated.

"Being in Egypt," he said, "not just being an Egyptian."

Mahmoud, however, had already forgotten what had passed and was thinking about something else.

"Ibrahim went there expecting to find the body, didn't he? That was where bodies came ashore. They even kept a pole there ready. He didn't expect it to be washed off again, either. That's not what happened. Once a body had grounded, you had to push it off. If there was any chance of it floating away again of its own accord, he wouldn't have bothered."

"So?"

"So it wasn't washed away. And he didn't push it off. So—"

"Yes?"

"Either somebody else did, which isn't likely, because what would be their motive? Ibrahim and the Chief had a motive all right; they wanted to get out of work. But anyone else?"

"Or?"

"Or somebody found it and took it away."

"Who would want to do a thing like that?"

"I think I know," said Mahmoud.

⟡

Mahmoud took Owen to a part of the city he had never been to before. It was tucked into a corner of Bulak and must have been near the river, for once Owen caught a glimpse of ship masts at the end of a street. But then streets disappeared altogether and there was just a mass of houses running into one another with the occasional alleyway between them.

The alleyways were scored with deep trenches down which the water ran when it rained; or would have run had its passage not been blocked by heaps of refuse, dung and animal guts, behind which the water collected in stagnant pools, above which mosquitoes hung in a cloud.

Mahmoud came to one of these alleyways and hesitated. Looking down it, Owen saw kite hawks picking at the carcass of a dog. Kites were Cairo's scavengers and kept the city clean. Owen normally took them for granted. Today, however, they seemed disturbing.

Mahmoud saw something further on and touched Owen's arm. In the shadow between the houses Owen could not see what it was but when they came up to it he saw that it was a man.

He was sitting against a wall with his legs tucked up under him. There was something odd about them. Perhaps he had no legs.

He seemed asleep. Mahmoud put his hand down and shook him. The man came awake with a start and put his hand up to his face. Owen had taken him for a Sudani because his face was black. As he raised his hand it seemed as if the whole front of his face came off. The blackness was a solid layer of flies. Beneath, the face was one raw wound.

"Which way?" said Mahmoud.

The man pointed to a kind of buttress beside him. Behind it was a long, thin alleyway. It was so narrow that as they went down it Owen's shoulders brushed the walls on each side. There was a trench running down this one, too, its contents so foul that he walked with his feet astride it. There was the soft scuttle of rats.

The alleyway opened out into a space between four houses. The houses were linked together with heavy fretwork windows so that you could not see the sky. Although it was midday everything was pitch dark. In the shadows something moved.

It looked like a dog. Owen thought of rabies and reached for his gun. Mahmoud sensed the movement and put out a restraining hand.

As Owen's eyes became accustomed to the dark he could see the dog more clearly. It wasn't a dog, it was more—he felt prickles on the back of his neck—like a hyena. Its head was down and its back sloped up into a kind of point at the rear.

Mahmoud spoke to it.

"Tell him that I have come," he said. "And that I bring a friend."

"Who is your friend?" asked a hoarse voice from the shadows.

"The Mamur Zapt."

There was a long silence.

"I will tell him."

The creature ran off on all fours.

"What the hell is this?" said Owen.

"Beggars. If they're not crippled to start with, they cripple themselves."

The creature came scuttling back. Owen could see now that it was a man. His back was horribly deformed and rose into a kind of hump at the base of the spine. His arms had been amputated at the elbows and his legs at the knees.

"Follow me," it said.

They went down an alleyway and in at a door. The room was dark but it was as if there was something fluttering in it. They went through it and on into another room where there was more daylight.

Mahmoud gave a cry of disgust and began to beat at his legs. He was black from shoes to waist.

Owen looked down at himself. He was black, too, as if coated with a layer of paint. And then he saw that the blackness was moving, and struck at it frantically.

He was covered with fleas.

There was a hoarse cackle of laughter.

Mahmoud strode across and kicked their guide heavily in the ribs.

"There was no need for this!" he said angrily.

The creature gave a gasp and slipped nimbly out of the way.

"You wanted to see the Man, didn't you?"

"Yes," said Mahmoud. "Where is he?"

The creature pointed to a dark opening in the wall.

Mahmoud went across and then beckoned Owen over.

They were looking down into a long dark cellar, lit by a brazier at one end. All round the room men were lying. In the middle of the room a small circle of men were passing something round. The air was heavy with the sweet smell of hashish.

"Who have we here?" said a deep voice.

"Greetings, Mustapha el-Gharbi," said Mahmoud.

He stepped down into the cellar. The circle opened and made space for them. Owen saw now what they were passing. It was the heavy coconut shell of the goza, or waterpipe, which was the way Cairo habitués preferred to take their hashish. He saw the charcoal glowing.

"Well, Mahmoud el Zaki," said the deep voice. "It is a long time since we saw you here."

Owen was able to pick out the speaker. It was a short, immensely fat man sitting opposite.

"It is a long time since my duties have called me here," said Mahmoud.

"That is because these days you are at the top of the ladder and it is other men who are sent to places like this."

"It is good for young men to come to places like this when they start," said Mahmoud. "Then they know what they are up against."

The man opposite chuckled.

"Still the same Mahmoud el Zaki," he said drily. "Unbending as ever. Nevertheless, he has come here, so he must seek a favor."

"Not necessarily a favor. A deal, rather."

"That's more like it. And," said the man, glaring at Owen, "you have brought a friend with you with whom indeed we might be able to do business."

"I don't think so. This is the Mamur Zapt."

"I know."

"Greetings, Mustapha el-Gharbi," said Owen.

"And to you greetings. It is a pleasure to have the Mamur Zapt with us again."

"Again?"

"I used to do business with one of your predecessors."

Which one was that? wondered Owen. The one who was dismissed for corruption?

He felt Mahmoud stiffen beside him.

"It is always good to do business with friends," he said diplomatically.

"That is so. And doubly good where pleasure and benefit coincide."

"Let us hope that is the case today. I am in the market for information."

"Is that so?" El-Gharbi stroked his beard. "What sort of information?"

"About a body that may have come ashore," said Mahmoud.

"What makes you think I might possess that kind of information?"

"Your people work the riverbanks. They are like ants or beetles. They work all day. And they do not miss much."

"They are good workers," said El-Gharbi, with the air of one making a concession.

"The body we are interested in came ashore in the Al-Gadira district four nights ago. It fetched up on a sandbank. The watchman went to tell the local Chief and when he came back the body was gone."

"Well, well," said El-Gharbi. "How puzzling for him."

"It puzzled me, too," said Mahmoud. "For your people do not usually take the body. They strip it and leave it."

"Bodies in themselves are usually worth nothing," said El-Gharbi.

"This one is worth something."

"How much?"

"That is what we have to determine."

"Tell me about this body."

"It is the body of a young girl. She was wearing pink shintiyan."

"Not a peasant woman, then. But then again, if she had been, you would not have been coming to see me. How did she come to be in the water?"

"We do not know. She was on a boat."

"Ah yes," said El-Gharbi. "Four nights ago? That would have been the Prince's dahabeeyah. Well, of course, that does put the price up."

"You have information, then, that might interest us?"

"I might. It is not straightforward, though."

"Would you be prepared to sell?"

"I might. The circumstances are, however, complex. And the price would have to be right. The market is, shall I say, a live one."

"What do you think would be the going price in such a market?"

"I would say that five thousand pounds, Egyptian, would attract interest."

"Alas," said Owen, "I feel that the largeness of spirit for which you are famous has expressed itself in the figure you give us."

"On the contrary. The affection I feel for you personally has led me, if anything, to understate it. The market is, as I have said, a live one."

As the negotiations proceeded, Owen became more and more convinced that this was so. El-Gharbi seemed to feel under no pressure at all to reduce his asking figure, and Owen felt that this was not just a matter of negotiating tactics. He seemed to be sure he would make his price.

The price was, however, out of Owen's reach. He had at his discretion a sum—a considerable sum, in the view of the Accounts Department—which could be used for the payment of informers. A sum like this, though, would eat such a hole in it as to jeopardize his ordinary work.

El-Gharbi was watching his face.

"Of course," he said, "if you were able to offer me something else—"

"Something else?" said Owen, puzzled. "What could that be?"

"Information. Like you, I am always in the market for information. And I, too, would pay a good price."

"What sort of information?"

"When wealth travels by river. Which boat. When it departs. Where it is going."

Owen shook his head.

"Alas," he said, "I do not sell that kind of information."

"Alas," El-Gharbi commiserated, "then it may be difficult for you to find the price my information commands in the market.

"There is always," said El-Gharbi after a while, "another possibility open to you. You yourself may not be able to raise the money. But perhaps you have friends who could—if it was important to them."

Owen's mind had begun to work on the same lines.

"My friends are, I am afraid, like myself, poor. But perhaps I should talk to them."

"Why not?" said El-Gharbi, smiling pleasantly. "I am sure your friends will be eager to help—once you explain to them what the money is for. Why not consult them? Only do not leave it too long. The market is, as I say, live. As opposed, of course, to the girl."

ᘒᨏᨏᘖ

"Five thousand pounds!" said the Prince, aghast. "That seems a lot of money."

"Yes. That's what I thought, too."

"It must be just a bargaining price. An opening offer. Pouf, man, you've let yourself be scared by a figure plucked out of the clouds. Go back and offer him five hundred."

"I have. And he wasn't interested."

"He *pretended* not to be interested, I daresay. But five hundred—well, that's a lot of money, too. For these people."

"He just laughed."

"A negotiating tactic. I am afraid you're not used to the ways of the bazaar, Captain Owen. You've let yourself be out-negotiated."

"I got the impression that the price was not negotiable."

"Oh, come! Any price is negotiable. It's just that you don't know how we do it here, Captain Owen. An Englishman—"

"Mr. el Zaki was with me."

The Prince looked at Mahmoud. "Was he? Well, he certainly ought to know better. Surely—"

"Captain Owen is as used to the ways of the bazaar as I am, Your Highness. He does, after all, negotiate daily with informers."

"Does he? Yes, well I suppose that's true. All the same, five thousand pounds! Surely that is excessive? What is the going rate for bodies in Cairo, Mr. el Zaki? Much less than that, I would have thought. Much, much less. Twenty pounds? Fifty pounds at most. A hundred, very exceptionally. Yes, I would have thought this was worth a hundred only."

"We are not exactly dealing in bodies," said Owen. "We are merely trying to buy information."

"Not even a body? And five thousand pounds! The price looks higher every time you speak, Captain Owen. I really do not think bargaining is your line. Information, you say? What information?"

Owen was forced to admit he did not exactly know.

"Well!" said the Prince. "Five thousand pounds is a lot of money to pay for something you do not exactly know."

"Before any money changed hands we would, of course, need to be satisfied that the information was worth it."

"I would certainly hope so! But, tell me, Captain Owen, what do you expect would be the nature of this information for which you are prepared to pay so high a price?"

Owen was silent.

Mahmoud was not, however.

"Marks on the body," he said. "How she died."

"I see."

The Prince considered the matter thoughtfully.

"Important as that is," he said, "I am not sure that it is worth five thousand pounds. Certainly not to me. After all, if what I think you are supposing is true, it would hardly be in my interest for such information to emerge. I speak hypothetically, of course."

"But look at it another way," said Owen. "If the information did not support what you think is Mr. el Zaki's view, would it not be helpful to know this? Would it not, as it were, clear the matter up? And might not that be worth five thousand pounds?"

"I do see your point. But I would regard that as a matter of public, not private interest. And I think, therefore, that the public should pay."

Owen tried in vain to convince him. The Prince was not to be persuaded.

He played one last card.

"Perhaps you are right," he said, with the air of one who had himself been convinced. "It *is* a public matter. The public should pay. Yes, I am sure you're right. I'll get on to it straightaway. It was just that—well, I thought you might have a special interest in what we found out—"

"Oh, I do! I do!"

"—and not wish it to be shared too widely. After all, it could be misinterpreted."

The Prince smiled.

"I think I can rely on you to see that it is not. After all, in view of the Special Agreement currently being discussed between the British government and the Egyptian government—"

"What Agreement is this?"

"You have not heard? Not even the Mamur Zapt? Well,"
said the Prince, "I do call that news management of the highest order. Obviously something there for you to study. Yes,
quite a lot there for you to study, I would say."

He accompanied them to the door. As they parted, he
clapped Owen on the back.

"Don't be downhearted, old fellow. It's all for the best.
You've been working jolly hard, I know. You and Mr. el Zaki."
The Prince's arm reached out to enfold Mahmoud. "But
you've both got more important things to do, I'm sure."

"I don't quite follow you."

"Well," said the Prince, "it's easy, isn't it? You've both been
working very hard—two of the best in the Khedive's service—
and you haven't been able to find anything. This—proposal
of yours, it's not going to come to anything, is it? I mean—
five thousand pounds is a lot of money. And for what? Some
highly dubious information? Not worth it. I'm sure everyone
will agree. So—"

"So what?"

"Is not this the time to drop the whole affair? It's really becoming rather tedious. Worse, now I come to think of it, a positive
drain on resources. Yes, that's it—a drain on the Government's
scarce resources. You see how quickly I pick up English ways
of talking. We must act responsibly. Time to call a halt."

"I am afraid, Your Highness," said Mahmoud stiffly, "that
once a case has been opened—"

"But *has* a case been opened, old fellow? A preliminary
investigation, certainly. But a case?"

"We make no such distinction."

"Oh, I am sure you do. A report comes in. You investigate.
You find there's nothing to it, a false rumor. So you drop it."

"I don't think this is like that."

"You don't? Well," said the Prince, smiling, "I'm not sure
I agree with you. No body, no case, I would have said. We'll
see, shall we?"

Zeinab had set it up for Owen to meet her theatrical friends
at their usual café and as she and Owen turned into the square,
there they were, occupying their usual tables on the edge of
the pavement.

Intellectual life in Cairo was conducted, as in Paris, in open-
air cafés. It was conducted, too, in French since France was
the country to which most of them owed intellectual alle-
giance. And the latest French journals were much in evidence.

There was one respect, however, in which it was very
unFrench. There were no women seated at the tables. Emanci-
pated as she considered herself, Zeinab would not have gone
up to them alone. Even with Owen, she attracted some
curious glances from people at adjoining tables. Women did
not do that kind of thing, even in cosmopolitan Cairo.

"Which was why Leila stood out," said one of Zeinab's
friends, Gamal.

Gamal was the playwright.

"Oh yes. I remember that evening. It was the first night
of *New Roses*, wasn't it? It had been so successful, *mon cher*—
the audience that first night was in rapture—that I thought
it would run and run. Alas!" He sighed heavily.

"It was the theme, Gamal," said someone across the table.
"It just wasn't popular." He turned to Owen. "The 'new roses'
were the emerging flowers of nationalism in the arts."

"I would have thought that would have been pretty
popular," said Zeinab.

"Nationalism, yes; the arts, no."

"That accounts for it," said Owen. "The first night you had all
the nationalists in Cairo. After that there was none left."

"Ah, my friend!" said Gamal, laughing reprovingly.

"And how did Leila come to be there?" asked Owen.
"Which of the aspects was she interested in?"

"Neither. She was interested in Suleiman."

"Suleiman?"

"He is here, I think, Suleiman! Where are you? Suleiman?"

Someone sitting at a table at the far end of the café got up and came over to them. He and Gamal embraced enthusiastically.

"Suleiman, there is someone I want you to meet." He introduced Owen. "A friend of mine. The Mamur Zapt."

"The Mamur Zapt?" said Suleiman, surprised but, so far as Owen could tell, not disconcerted. "What friends you have, Gamal!"

They shook hands and Suleiman pulled a chair up.

"He wants to know about Leila," said Gamal.

"Leila?" Suleiman made a face. "This is a shaming thing for me, Gamal. It is not kind of you."

"Why be ashamed?" asked Gamal. "Is not love a thing to be proud of?"

"It is, when it is love. But I am not sure it was love, not on my side at least."

"She loved you?" said Zeinab.

"Well, yes, I think so. And at first I felt flattered— I don't usually have an effect on women like that—and thought I loved her. But then..."

"You fell out of love?"

"Well, no. It was just that she became—tiresome, really, she was so clinging. And then I thought: It is not I she finds special, any responsive man would do, it is the fact of being in love she finds special. I am not expressing myself very well."

"Being in love *is* special for women," said Zeinab.

"Yes, yes. I realize that, but I think that also there has to be one man particularly who means something special to you—"

"There were other men?"

"No, no. I did not mean that. I meant, I think, that it is very important to Leila, or it was then, to have a man, simply have a man. Any man would do, it didn't have to be me. It was as if she was desperate—No, no, I didn't mean that. What a terrible thing to say! I meant—"

"She needed love and protection," said Zeinab.

"Yes," said Suleiman, downcast. "Yes, I am sure you are right. Only—I'm not very good at that sort of thing. I—I want to get on with my work."

"Suleiman is a sculptor," said Gamal.

"Well, I am trying to be," said Suleiman modestly. "Not very successfully, I am afraid. But I did have the chance of an exhibition, and it was just at that time, and I was working hard, and she—she, well, I suppose she was a distraction."

"Is it just that he is like you?" Zeinab asked Owen. "Or are all men like this?"

"I don't know about that," said Gamal. "But I know that if you are an artist, that is how it is."

"It is not art that needs new roses," said Zeinab, "it is the way men see women."

Owen hurriedly intervened.

"At any rate," he said, "you felt less warmly towards her than you had done."

"Yes. But she wouldn't let me go. She clung."

"What do you expect?" said Zeinab. "A woman's love is not like a man's. Once you give it, you can't take it back."

"She pursued you?"

"Yes. Everywhere I went."

"And that was how she came to be at the reception?"

"What reception is this?"

"The first night of Gamal's play, *New Roses*. There was a reception afterwards."

"I remember it. Was she there? Yes, I think she was there."

"Was she invited?"

"No one was invited," said Gamal. "It just happened."

"She tagged along."

"Did she come with you?"

"No. I don't think she came with anyone. But when I came into the room, there she was. And I thought: There she is again! Will I never be rid of her? This is what I am ashamed of," said Suleiman. "It was unkind."

"Did you speak to her?"

"No. I tried to avoid her. In fact, I did avoid her. She did not speak to me."

"Was that because she was speaking to someone else?"

"I do not know."

There was a general appeal around the tables.

"Who did Leila speak to at the *New Roses* party?"

One or two names were suggested.

"The Prince, I think," said someone.

"Narouz?"

"Yes. It was the only thing he found interesting during the evening, I think."

"The man is a Philistine," declared Gamal.

"What was he doing there, anyway?"

"Raoul was trying to tap him for money."

"Some hope. He's only interested in car racing."

"Women?" asked Owen.

"Leila, certainly. They went off together. Sorry, Suleiman."

"I don't mind," said Suleiman. "In fact, it's a relief."

"How did you get to know her?"

"She turned up, didn't she, at one of our soirées?" He appealed to the group.

"Faisal brought her."

"Who is Faisal?"

"Oh, he's not one of us. He hung around us for a while. He thought he was interested in the arts. One of those rich men, you know, no talent, no dedication. He went off to France."

"And Leila?"

"Leila stayed. She started going around with—who was it? That journalist."

"Hargazy?"

"That's right. She went around with him for a while. Off and on. I don't know when it stopped."

"When she took up with Suleiman."

"She was always tagging along with someone."

"What else could she do?" asked Zeinab with asperity.

"Did she have any other friends?" asked Owen.

"I wouldn't have thought so. Judging by the amount of time she spent with us."

"Why all these questions?" asked someone.

"Because she's dead," said Zeinab.

"Dead?"

They were shocked.

"When was this? Are you sure? I saw her only recently," said Gamal.

"It was Tuesday," said Zeinab. "Tuesday when she was killed."

"We don't know that for cert—" began Owen, but his voice was drowned in the barrage of questions, cries of concern and comment.

"But that is awful!"

"Leila! I cannot believe it!"

"I didn't know her well, but—somehow one had got used to her."

"None of us knew her well, I suppose."

"Didn't any of you ever talk to her?" demanded Zeinab.

"Of course we did. We all spoke to her."

"That's not the same thing. Did you ever talk to her in the way she wanted? Needed?"

"Suleiman did."

"I'm not sure I did," said Suleiman thoughtfully, "now."

Zeinab was very quiet afterwards as she and Owen drove home in an arabeah. Cairo was at its most magical. The streets were still and cool and silver in the moonlight. The shadows of the minarets made gentle curves in the dust and when Owen looked up, there they were, graceful against the deep blue of the Egyptian night. He bent over and kissed her.

Zeinab kissed him back mechanically. She was thinking about Leila.

"She was very alone, wasn't she?"

"If you leave home you are alone."

"If you're a woman," said Zeinab.

"She must have wanted to leave home terribly badly. Maybe I ought to take a look at her family."

"Perhaps it wasn't so much that she wanted to leave home. Perhaps it was more that she just wanted to be somewhere else. Be someone else."

Later, she looked up at him. The moonlight was on her face and he could see her clearly.

"You are going to do something about it, aren't you?" she said.

The next morning, though, he found a message on his desk from Paul, asking if they could meet for a drink at lunchtime at the Club.

They took their drinks out on to the verandah where they would not be disturbed.

"I'm not following you," said Owen, bewildered. "I thought you *wanted* me to stay close to it?"

"Not *so* close. Keep a gentle eye on it from afar."

"Well, fine. I can do that," said Owen, shrugging his shoulders. "It's Mahmoud's pigeon really. I'm just there to see, well, that it doesn't build up into anything major."

"That's right." Paul nodded approvingly. "We wouldn't want that, so continue keeping an eye on it. But from afar. No need to involve yourself directly. Ease off a bit. I'm sure you've got plenty of other things to do."

"I have, yes. There's a lot on just at the moment. But— I'm still a bit puzzled. I thought this was important?"

"Well, hardly. Certainly not in itself. An accident, a murder— they come with the ice cream in Cairo. It was just that this could have had political implications."

"And you don't think that's likely now?"

"I think there are more important political considerations."

"Well, fine, you would know. Mahmoud will be getting on with it anyway. He doesn't need me."

For all Paul's highly developed, possibly overdeveloped, political sense, he was normally straight with Owen. After all, he explained, politics wasn't everything—what about drink, for instance?—and if you couldn't be trusted to call properly when you were playing tennis, who would want to play with you?

Now he was toying uncomfortably with his glass.

"I have a feeling," he said at last, "that Mahmoud may be receiving the same sort of advice."

"To back off? What's going on?" Light dawned. "You can't—you don't mean to say you're giving in to Narouz?"

"Certainly not! Narouz is just a sideshow, a distraction. The fact is, though, that we could do without a distraction just now."

"It's this Special Agreement, is it?"

"How do you know about that? It's supposed to be top, pinnacle-top, secret. Only the Consul-General and the Khedive are supposed to know."

"*You* know."

"I am the right side of the Consul-General's brain. How do *you* know?"

"I have access to the left side of the Khedive's brain."

"You keep your spies in peculiar places, Gareth."

"I do. But they didn't tell me about this. Nor that you were giving in to Narouz."

"We're *not* giving in to Narouz. It's just that we don't want anything to ruffle the Khedive's hair just when the negotiations are approaching a delicate stage."

"Narouz is a sideshow. You said it yourself."

"The Khedive will have to carry his family with him. Potential heirs, at least. The Treaty is to do with a possible extension of the British presence here in return for continuing political support. And cash, of course."

"And Narouz is one of the heirs?"

"Potential. Only potential."

"So you don't want us to press this case?"

"Are you in a position to press a case?"

"No, not yet."

"Why don't you just leave it like that? Let it roll along, latent, so to speak. It'll mean we've got a hold over him. We might use it sometime."

"I don't know if Mahmoud will play."

"I don't think Mahmoud will have any option. Not if he's formally taken off the case."

"I don't know that I want to play, either."

"Now, Gareth, no moral heroics, *please!*"

"It's not moral heroics, it's Zeinab. She's rather got the bit between her teeth on this."

"Zeinab? How the hell does she come to be involved? She's not a friend of the girl, is she?"

"No. Has friends who are. It's not that. It's—well, an abstract principle of justice, I suppose."

"Oh, come, Gareth! Zeinab's not interested in an abstract anything! A more concrete, realistic girl I've never met. Emotional, perhaps, but—"

"She's pretty emotionally involved here."

"How the hell did she get to be emotionally involved? How the hell did she get to be involved anyway? Gareth! You've been talking to her! Is that it?"

"A bit."

"You daft idiot! Couldn't you see that she would get emotionally involved?"

"We've talked about things before."

"About girls trying to strike out alone in Egypt? I'll bet you haven't."

"It has not arisen," said Owen stiffly.

"Can you imagine Zeinab talking about a thing like that and *not* getting emotionally involved? Zeinab would get emotionally involved if she was talking about breakfast."

"We've got to talk about something, haven't we?"

"Your work? That the sort of thing you talk about in bed, Gareth? You worry me. You sound more and more like—I've got to say it—yes, a *husband*, Gareth."

"I don't think things have got quite as far as that yet."

"They seem to me to be drifting that way. And if they are, then I think you want to think about it, Gareth. Because I can see problems. Zeinab's a lovely girl, but—"

"For Christ's sake, Paul!"

"I know, I know. All the same—"

"Let's get off the relationships. You were giving me instructions."

"*Advice*, I was giving you. *Advice*."

"Advice. Back off the investigation. Leave it all alone. Let Narouz get away with it."

"That was *not* my advice. Timing was what I was talking about. And the balance between political and personal priorities."

"I get the message."

"I hope you do. Especially the bit about balance."

"I do. But will Zeinab?"

Chapter 6

"No," said Zeinab.

"Look, let's not be too hasty—"

"I do not understand. First you are on this case, then you are off. One moment you give all your time to it, you don't come home till late at night, you don't even come home in the afternoon like ordinary men, the next you are giving no time to it at all. Is it the same man, I ask myself?"

"Of course it's the same man. It's just that—"

"Don't you care at all what you do? Or is it that your feelings suddenly alter? They switch and change all the time, phu! like this. You are," said Zeinab, "emotionally erratic."

"It's nothing to do with emotion—"

"Oh?" said Zeinab, bridling. "You don't care about Leila? You don't care about a poor girl, alone and brutally murdered? You have no feeling? Is that it?"

"No, that's not it. Of course I care. But—"

"She is only a woman, is that it?" said Zeinab, firing up. "An Egyptian woman, yes? What is a mere Egyptian woman to the mighty British? They brush her aside, yes, like a fly."

"Calm down, calm down! I am very concerned—"

"Concern! Pah! Is that all? I am concerned too. I am concerned that you have a heart of stone. I am concerned that with you one minute it is this, the next it is that. I am concerned that the man who is here today is not the same as the man who was here yesterday. I—"

"OK, OK." This was going to be as difficult as he had imagined. "It's not me that changes," he said mildly. "It's just that—well, circumstances change."

"And you change with them, yes? Just like that. Something happens and immediately you change."

"No. It's not like that."

"It's not? Well, it seems to me just like that. We talk, we agree, I go away and start doing something, and then suddenly it's all different. It all changes. You blow hot, you blow cold. You go to bed saying one thing, you wake up saying another."

"It's not like that."

"Oh, isn't it? I am glad. Because I thought perhaps it was the same with me. Now you love me, now you don't."

"You know I love you."

"But that," said Zeinab, "is precisely what I don't know. Now that we have all this change. You loved me yesterday, or so I believed. Yes, I believed you. But tomorrow? Will you love me then?"

The large dark eyes stared at him tragically. Owen, who had suspected that Zeinab was enjoying the drama, melted totally.

"Of course I will!"

"You say it," said Zeinab somberly, "as if you meant it. But then, you spoke about Leila in that way too."

"That's different."

"Oh? Why is it different?"

"That—well, that's work."

"I do not make that distinction," said Zeinab.

"At work you've got to go along with things more. You're subject to pressures."

"I see."

She sat there silently for a few moments. Owen hoped that she was calming down.

"That's it, is it?" she said suddenly.

"What?"

"Pressure."

"Arguments, rather."

"And you have been persuaded by these arguments?"

"Yes."

"Well, I haven't," said Zeinab.

"You haven't heard them," Owen pointed out.

"You won't tell me them. You can't," said Zeinab, "tell me them. And do you know why? Because they are British arguments. They are not my arguments, they are not even your arguments. They are British arguments."

She suddenly dissolved into floods of tears.

"I hate you!" she said. "I hate you!"

"Oh, look—"

"No. Don't touch me. It is not the man I love who touches me, it is the British."

"You mustn't see it like that!"

"I see it like that because it is like that."

"It is not like that."

"No? Tell me then: are you going to do what they say?"

"Well—"

"You see," said Zeinab.

⁂

Mahmoud had a case that morning in the Mixed Tribunals and Owen wanted to send a letter to England so they agreed to meet at noon at the Post Office.

Mahmoud wasn't there when he arrived, so he went inside to buy his stamps and then came out to use the wet roller hanging against the wall. The heat tended to dry up the gum on stamps and getting them to stick on was the very devil.

Facing the front of the Post Office was a long row of seal-makers and scribes squatting in the dust with their customers. The ordinary Egyptian could not write and if he wished to send a letter he would have to get a scribe to write it for him. And since he could not sign it he would use a seal.

Owen wondered suddenly whether Leila had been able to write. Almost certainly not, for few women could. How, then, did Narouz communicate with her? If by note, then she would have had to get a scribe to read it to her. But perhaps Narouz sent a messenger.

In either case the man would know the message: and in either case they ought to be able to find him. But he was forgetting.

Mahmoud came out of the Mixed Tribunals and crossed the street towards him. He was carrying a huge bundle of papers and didn't want to walk far, so they went into the Arab café beside the Post Office.

Mahmoud dumped the papers on a chair and sat down with relief. He had, he told Owen, been on his feet all morning.

"Did you get anywhere?"

"No," said Mahmoud. "The usual."

The Egyptian system of courts was one of the most complicated in the world. Foreigners in Egypt received considerable legal privileges. In some cases they could be tried only by their own national courts and cases had to be remitted to Smyrna or Ankara or wherever it was. In other cases, where an Egyptian national was involved as well as a foreigner, the case had to be sent to the Mixed Courts, where the law was different from that in the ordinary Egyptian courts. The possibilities for evasion were endless.

Owen commiserated.

Mahmoud shrugged his shoulders.

"You get used to it," he said.

He was, understandably, not very cheerful this morning.

"Yes," he said, "they told me yesterday."

"What did they tell you? To drop it?"

"No, no. They wouldn't do that. If a case is closed, you've got to say why. Sometimes," said Mahmoud, "bureaucracy has its uses."

"What did they tell you, then?"

"Basically, to leave it alone for a while. A long, long while. To concentrate on something else. That's why," said Mahmoud, tapping the bundle of papers, "they've given me this. I had to get it all up last night. I've got another one for tomorrow. And the day after. I don't think," he said, "they trust me to do nothing."

He laughed, but it was an injured, bitter laugh. If you were a Parquet lawyer you got used to cases getting nowhere; but that didn't mean you liked it.

"It's Narouz, isn't it?" he said. "He's fixed it."

Owen nodded.

"Well," said Mahmoud, "it was always on the cards. He's a member of the Royal Family. They wouldn't want to go too close to the Khedive. What I can't understand, though, is why the British should want to get involved."

"They don't want to get involved. All they want to do is make sure it doesn't blow up into anything."

"For the sake of the Khedive?"

"Certainly not for the sake of Narouz."

Mahmoud, fortunately, did not probe.

"I wouldn't have thought they'd have bothered," he said.

It was the custom in Egypt, on the Friday after a body had been interred, for the women of the family to visit the tomb, where they would break a palm branch over the grave and distribute cakes and bread to the poor.

When Ali Marwash's daughter died the custom was followed to the letter since the girl was Ali Marwash's only child and he cared for her more than he probably would have had done had there been sons in the family.

The mourners went to the tomb and a fiki, a professional holy reader, especially hired for the occasion, chanted the appropriate verses from the Koran. The palm branch was broken and placed on the grave and the cakes and bread distributed.

The party was about to depart when the mother of the dead girl noticed that the earth over the entrance to the tomb had been disturbed, and when she looked more closely she saw that one of the roofing stones had been moved.

Grave-robbing in Egypt was a traditional pursuit and she immediately feared the worst. Ali Marwash was not a rich man, but he had loved his daughter and had wrapped her in a Kashmir shawl before interring her.

It was normal to tear the shawl first so that its value would not tempt a profane person to violate the tomb; but the shawl had been a beautiful one and he had not been able to bring himself to do that. His wife now feared that they had been punished for his presumption.

Her screams attracted a large crowd and the fiki, taking control, sent someone to fetch her husband. A sheikh was summoned and with his authority and before a vast concourse of onlookers the tomb was reopened.

The mother's fears were realized, for the tomb had indeed been violated. Her daughter's body had been removed altogether. And in its place, stacked high in the subterranean vault, was a large pile of guns and ammunition.

The police were called at once and the District Chief of Police, whose recent experiences had reinforced a strong natural tendency towards caution, sent immediately for the Mamur Zapt.

By the time Owen arrived the crowd was sixty deep and he had to get his constables to clear a way through.

The tomb consisted of an oblong brick vault with an arched roof high enough to allow a person buried in it to sit up with care when visited by the two examining angels, Munkar and Nekeer. On top of this was a solid brick monument with an upright stone. The entrance was through a small separate cell to the northeast, and it was this which had been tampered with.

Owen stepped down into the cell, bent and looked through the doorway into the burial vault. At first he could not see anything, but then someone pushed a lighted torch in front of him and he caught the gleam of the bluish-gray metal inside.

It was a large cache of arms. He pulled one out. It was a rifle in pristine condition, still greasy from the packing case and with the heavy, cold distinctive smell he knew so well.

The man holding the torch was, he saw now, one of the local constables he had used on the arms search.

"Is this it, effendi?" said the man excitedly.

Owen slipped his hand in again and felt around on the floor. His hand closed around an object. He pulled it out and looked at it. It was a clip of ammunition, exactly similar to those left behind in the kuttub in the fountain house.

🙰

"Oh, good," said Garvin, "I was afraid you'd forgotten about things like that, with your recent preoccupations."

He was, nevertheless, in a genial mood this morning. A bearer slipped in behind Owen and stood up a gun in the corner behind Garvin's desk. That accounted for it. It was a sporting gun.

"Bag anything this morning?"

"Two hare and a hoopoe."

"Hoopoe?"

"It happened to be there so I potted it."

It was possible to get good, though restricted, shooting within an hour's ride from Cairo and sometimes Garvin went out in the early morning before coming to the office. For duck you needed really to go north, to the big lakes around Alexandria and, of course, for big game you had to go south. But hare and even the odd gazelle were available locally.

Like many of the British, Garvin brought his past with him. He was the son of a "squarson," a country parson who had the standing and habits of a squire. Garvin had been brought up to hunting and shooting, skills which in the opinion of the Consul-General exactly equipped a young man for a career in the Ministry of the Interior.

Those and one other: facility at learning Arabic. Cromer had expected all his staff to speak Arabic fluently and Garvin, after twenty years in Egypt, spoke the language like a native. He also knew the country like a native.

"Oh, good," said Owen.

"Foolish of them," said Garvin. "They must have known the women would be back."

"I don't think they meant to leave them there," said Owen. "They had to move them in a hurry when my people started going through the district and it was just intended as a temporary hiding place. My guess is that they meant to come back, only with so much police activity they didn't like to risk it."

"So all that faffing around actually achieved something?"

"The operation was successful, yes. The trouble is," said Owen, "that it was only partly successful. We got the arms but not the men."

"Well, at least it means that if we're shot, it'll be by another lot of guns. That's something."

"There'll be other shipments. We've got to get the men. So I'm keeping some people down in Al-Gadira."

"They'll be miles away by now," said Garvin.

"I don't know that they will. My hunch is that they're local. Why did they move the arms in the first place? Because they saw the search coming their way. That suggests they were in the area. What did they do? They moved them out of the way but not out of the district, just to somewhere handy where they could easily pick them up. That suggests they were local, too."

Garvin nodded his head in acknowledgment.

"Who have you got down there?"

"Georgiades."

"He's all right," said Garvin.

"Yes. There's another thing, too. While he's down there he can keep his eyes open generally. There seems to be a lot happening in Al-Gadira just now."

He told Garvin about Leila.

"That girl?" said Garvin. "I thought you were dropping that?"

"I'm distancing myself. But I couldn't help noticing that was Al-Gadira too."

"Coincidence," said Garvin dismissively.

"Maybe. But she lived there and she died there."

"Her body was washed up there. That's not the same thing."

"It's what happened to her body."

"Halfway to Alexandria by now, I would say."

"Well," said Owen, "it might not be."

"Does it matter?" asked Garvin.

"Yes," said Owen. He found it difficult to pick the right words. Everything that came to mind seemed inappropriate. He wanted to say "untidy" but that was ridiculously inappropriate. Then he wanted to say that you couldn't have bodies floating around but "floating," in the circumstances, was hardly the word.

"It might pop up at an awkward moment," he said, which was hardly any better.

"We'll have to risk that," said Garvin briskly.

Owen was deliberating whether this was the moment. Garvin seemed fairly amenable this morning. He might never have a better chance.

"I wonder if we're handling this in the right way," he said cautiously.

He didn't need to work through Garvin. Although Garvin was shown as his formal superior in terms of the office organization chart, that was to some extent a convenient fiction and the Mamur Zapt had his own lines of communication to the powers that were.

Garvin, however, played bridge with the Consul-General and was a member of his social circle. The habit of the British

overseas was to replicate the governing patterns of the
Establishment in London, with its loose formal structure and
very tight informal one, articulated through a wide variety
of social occasions, and Egypt was no exception.

Owen was, he was aware, a hired man and not a member
of the charmed social circle and if he wanted to get things
done he had to do it indirectly by tweaking the inner social
system.

"What do you mean?" said Garvin, looking at him sharply.

"Letting Narouz block it. It's bound to get out and then
it will look as if we're helping the Khedive to cover up. Is
that a good idea?"

"He's the Government, isn't he?"

"Yes, but this kind of thing gives the Government a bad
name. Do we want to be all that closely identified with the
Government over a thing like this?"

"A thing like *what*?"

"Corruption. Possible murder."

"What are you saying?"

"I'm saying we should let Mahmoud go on investigating
this case. Seriously, I mean."

Garvin looked at him searchingly, then looked away.

"There are one or two things on at the moment," he said.

"I know. The Agreement."

"Well, then."

"I don't see that the two have to go together."

"They go together," said Garvin, "because the only legal
basis we have for being in Egypt is that we're here by the
Khedive's invitation. It's a personal thing, there's no formal
treaty or anything like that. It's just his invitation. And he's
prepared to renew it, provided we're prepared to look after
him and see he stays in power."

"Would a thing like this stop him from staying in power?"

"It might."

"We don't have to do *everything* he wants," said Owen,
exasperated.

"Certainly not. But we do have to do everything he wants for the next month or so."

"I was hoping," said Owen, "that you might be able to have a word—"

"I'm afraid not," said Garvin.

᠗

"This is unreasonable," said Owen.

"On the contrary," said Zeinab. "You don't love me; so why should we make love?"

"I do love you."

"You don't listen to me," said Zeinab, "let alone love me."

"I am doing what I can. I've been trying to persuade them—"

"Persuade them?" said Zeinab incredulously. "Do you have to persuade people to do what is obviously right?"

"They don't see it like that. They—"

"Why do you always have to take their point of view?"

"I am not taking their point of view. I am working within it."

"I do not follow these sophistries," said Zeinab.

"If I do it too directly they won't listen to me."

"They don't listen to you. You don't listen to me. It is time," said Zeinab, "that the whole lot of you started listening."

"Listen—"

"*I*," said Zeinab, "always listen."

"No, you don't. Try and hear what I am saying. I *am* doing something about it, I *am* trying to get them to change their mind. I am spending about all my time on the bloody thing—"

"Leila," said Zeinab. "Is that what you mean?"

"The case. And it's not even my case. I am not really on it. It's not really anything to do with me."

"An injustice occurs," said Zeinab, "and it's not really anything to do with you?"

"I'm just trying to do a job. I am not trying to put the whole world right. That's something God can do."

"The old Mamur Zapt," said Zeinab, "would have listened."

"The old Mamur Zapt was a crook."

"And had a weakness for women. There are," said Zeinab, "many similarities between you. Nevertheless—"

"Look, in the old days the Mamur Zapt was responsible for bloody everything in the city. My role is more circumscribed."

"Call yourself Mamur Zapt and you can't do anything when the woman you claim you love pleads to you for justice?"

"Look, I'm just concerned with political things—"

"Ah!" said Zeinab. "There we have it!"

"Yes. And that's not the same thing as ordinary criminal offenses. Why don't you go to the Parquet?"

"The Parquet," said Zeinab, "is not political, no? I thought you told me they were a bunch of political, fix-it lawyers? I thought you told me that everything is in the end political? Ah, I see! It is another of these now-it-is, now-it-isn't things. Like your love!"

"No," said Owen. "Not like my love at all."

"Ah, but I think it is! And so," said Zeinab, "since you do not love me, properly, not truly, not the way I love you, it would not be right for us to make love."

"All right, then," said Owen, getting up. "If you feel like that."

"I do feel like that. And my feelings are not changeable like yours. I shall feel the same tomorrow."

"Bloody hell!"

"And every day, in fact. Until you have made your mind up. The right way, of course."

༄

"Well, that *is* a problem!" said Paul. "Should it have priority over the future of the British Empire, though? Ordinarily I would say yes without hesitation. On this occasion, however—"

They were sitting outside on the verandah. Stretching into the distance were the various sports fields of the Club. Far away a hockey match was in progress. The standard of hockey was good. Most officials in Egypt and all the army had served in India.

Because of the heat, matches were played in the late afternoon. They had to start promptly at four, however, since the twilight came early in Egypt and by six it was getting too dark to see.

There were tennis courts as well. Because you lost so much body water in the heat, small boys brought tumblers of iced water at the end of every set. Even so, by the end of a match you were seriously depleted and most players repaired to the bar to rebuild their resources.

"We must look for a compromise," said Paul.

"I don't think Zeinab goes in for compromises much," said Owen gloomily. "It's all or nothing with her. At the moment it's nothing."

"You mustn't give up," said Paul firmly. "We've got the best brains in Egypt on this. Yours and mine."

"Where politics is concerned," said Owen, "that is probably true. In your case, at any rate. In things like this, though—"

"All problems are in the end political. Wasn't that what you said she said?"

"She said I said it."

"And it was very perceptive of you. So let's treat this as a political problem and look for a political solution."

"No, no, no, no. It won't work, I tell you. The only thing that would help would be if we could finish off this Leila business."

"There you are! I told you the problem was a political one."

"Yes, and you also told me, yesterday, that you couldn't do a thing about it."

"That was yesterday and I was solving a different problem then."

Paul, looking over the fields, considered the matter. There was an indignant shout from the hockey players. A hawk had swooped low over the field of play, picked up the ball in its claws and flown off with it. The ball, however, was too big for it and dropped from its clutch. The referee retrieved it and ordered a bully-off.

"We must do something about those birds," said Paul. "They're becoming a problem."

"Is there a political solution for that, too?" asked Owen.

"Firepower," said Paul, undisconcerted. "War is the extension of politics by other means."

"I don't think that will help with Zeinab."

"Compromise," said Paul. "That's what we've got to go for."

"I tell you Zeinab isn't interested in compromise."

"She adopts a strong negotiating position."

"No, no, it's not like that, Paul. She means what she says."

"Heavens! Unorthodox, too! That *does* require some thought."

A whistle blew and the match ended. The hockey players trooped off and began to make their way back towards the clubhouse.

"The only way forward I can see," said Paul, "is to distribute the problem through time."

"*What!*"

"Yes, that's it. It's simpler than I had thought. In political terms, that is. It's just a straightforward bargaining situation distributed over time."

"What the hell are you talking about, Paul?"

"You see, Zeinab's not going to move until the Leila business gets settled. The Leila business is not going to get settled until the Agreement gets signed. (I mean, afterwards who cares a damn what Narouz thinks or does?) So all you've got to do is wait for the Agreement to get signed. Then you can get going on the case. And then, when you've got that sorted out, things will get sorted out with Zeinab, too."

"How long is all that going to take?"

"Oh, if there's no hiccup in the negotiations, the Agreement will be signed within a couple of months or so."

"You mean wait a couple of *months*? And then sort the case out? And only then—?"

"We all have to make sacrifices, Gareth."

⟨⟩

By about ten in the morning the sun was already dazzlingly bright and all living objects were seeking the shade. One of the orderlies came round closing the shutters. The room was plunged into darkness and stayed like that for the rest of the day.

At first it was cool and rather pleasant but as the day wore on, the temperature in the room rose. You opened the door into the corridor but not the window into the sun and that way you got—but perhaps this was fancy—a draft of air.

There were fans suspended from the ceilings in each of the rooms but in Owen's view all they did was to move hot air from one place to another and he very rarely switched his on. Besides, they blew the papers all over the place.

This morning was papers. He had a pile on his desk which he was working systematically through; reports from agents, neatly docketed and summarized by Nikos, offensive memoranda from the Finance Department, irrelevant offerings from Personnel and aggrieved submissions from the Khedive, the Kadi, the Mufti and all the others who considered that the Mamur Zapt was exceeding his powers.

He pushed them all aside. On the end of the desk was a heap of newspapers. The ones he had were in Arabic, French and English. The ones in Italian, Greek, Armenian, Turkish and Amharic would go to other people in the office. Cairo was a polyglot community and had a lively press.

Too lively on occasion. One of the Mamur Zapt's duties was to read the press before publication and excise any passage he considered inflammatory. Censorship? Call it ensuring that people's feelings were not offended.

He picked up one of the newspapers and began reading. It was the influential *Al-Liwa*, nationalist in sympathies and radical in tone. Also windy rhetorical in tone. It was heavy going. His attention wandered.

What was he going to do? He had tried all his usual lines, Paul, Garvin, others, the ones he always used when he wanted to get official policy reversed or amended, and he had got nowhere. The Administration, this time, was showing unusual unanimity.

Obviously, the Agreement mattered. Well, he didn't mind that; it mattered to him, too. He wanted to stay in Egypt, didn't he? And, unfortunately, that meant going along with the Khedive. They were there by his invitation and only by his invitation. The other powers didn't like it—they wanted Britain to get out of Egypt—but so long as the fiction could be maintained that the British were there at the express request of the Egyptian sovereign, there was not much they could do about it.

Owen was all for the Agreement. He was also, on the whole, for the Khedive on the grounds that at least he was the devil they knew. True, there were some things he didn't like about the Khedive's regime, the patronage, the corruption, the inefficiency. He could understand the desire of people like Mahmoud for reform and change.

Well, they could certainly have change. The British Government in London, the Administration itself in Egypt, was committed to Progress. Within limits, of course. But it had to be gradual, orderly change, sensible reform, rather on the British model. He was all in favor of that.

And there was no real discrepancy, either, between that—in general—and the Agreement.

It was only when they got down to the particular that problems arose. And Zeinab, unfortunately, tended to think in terms of the particular. It must be something to do, he decided, with her lack of a formal education.

She was very difficult to reason with. He couldn't see much hope that way.

But nor could he see much hope any other way. He had tried all other things he knew. Everywhere, the way was blocked.

What was he going to do?

And then, as his eye flicked mechanically over the page, it caught something tucked away at the bottom of one of the columns.

Chapter 7

"How did they get hold of that?" said Garvin.

"I could ask them," said Owen, "but would that be a good idea?"

"No," said Garvin, pushing the newspaper back to him, "I suppose you are right."

"It would just give it more prominence. They would know they were onto something."

"You're not going to let it go out, though?"

"No, I've cut it, along with a lot of other passages. It's just one among many. They may think it's just because it contains a reference to the Khedive's family."

Garvin looked at the passage again.

"I don't think they'll think that," he said.

"Then what would you suggest we do?"

"I'll have to take advice," said Garvin.

He drummed his fingers on his desk.

"Owen," he said, "doesn't this come a bit pat?"

"What do you mean?"

"You've been trying to get us not to hush this case up."

"I've been trying to get you not to block it."

"Same thing. I was wondering—"

"If I'd leaked this myself?"

"Did you?"

"No."

"It falls a little conveniently."

Owen shrugged. He picked up the newspaper and read the passage again. It read:

> A young woman, Miss Leila Sekhmet, was drowned in the river last week. Apparently, she fell off a boat. That is strange, for the boat was moored for the night and the river was calm. What is even stranger is that the boat was a dahabeeyah under the hire of Prince Narouz. What was a young, unmarried girl doing at night on the Prince's dahabeeyah, we wonder? And what happened, that a girl should fall overboard? The Parquet are investigating.

"It would be interesting to know how they got it," he said. "The information is good."

"So good," said Garvin, "that—"

"I must have given it them?" Owen smiled. "I might have," he said, "if I'd thought of it. But even if I did, we're still left with the same question: what are we going to do about it?"

ᏎᏇᏇᎧ

"It's put the cat among the pigeons," said Paul. "It really has. You're sure you're nothing to do with it?"

"Cross my heart."

"I'm all for sharp maneuvers, Gareth, but I like to be on the inside of them."

"Haven't I always kept you on the inside of them?"

"So long as it stays like that."

"It'll stay like that. Anyway, I don't go in for sharp maneuvers much myself. I always come to you for them."

Paul sighed.

"Why do I allow myself to be persuaded by this unscrupulous Welsh Levantine?" he asked.

A suffragi went by carrying two sherry glasses on a silver tray. Paul intercepted him.

"Which for you?" he asked Owen. "Pale or medium?"

"Pale."

"I feel pale. You can have the medium."

"Would the effendi prefer sweet?" asked the suffragi.

"No, thanks. The world isn't very sweet just at the moment."

The Consul-General's agents, fresh from England, might not have been prepared to agree with him. There was a near-Indian opulence about the proceedings. The light from the heavy gilt chandelier overhead sparkled on the silverware: little ornate Persian boxes of sweets and cigarettes, huge Arabesque trays of silver and bronze, the filigree of dainty caskets, the solider work of massive fruit bowls, the trays of the turbanned, red-sashed suffragis gliding round with drinks.

The reception was being held in the main hall of the Residency. The marble floor was already crowded with guests. Knots of expatriates had gathered around each visitor, eager for news from England. Senior Egyptians from the Ministries talked quietly among themselves. Practiced diplomats from the embassies circulated among the groups.

Normally Paul would have been circulating with the best of them, oiling the wheels. The moment Owen had come in, however, he had waylaid him and taken him off behind the potted palms.

"Well," he said, "if it's not you, it's serious."

"I'm glad you put it like that," said Owen. "Garvin put it the other way: if it *was* me, there'd be trouble."

"Oh, that too," said Paul, waving a hand dismissively.

"But you're right. It *is* serious. It's bound to get out now. I've stopped it this time but it will come out somewhere else. In one of the illegal papers. The point is, they've spotted it. And once that has happened, it's only a matter of time."

A group began to form on the other side of the potted palms. A tall Egyptian looked over, saw Paul and waved his hand. Paul waved back. A short, plump man in tails peered round the edge of the plants.

"My God!" he said. "The Mamur Zapt! Plotting, as usual."

"But not against you this time, Chargé," said Owen in French. "We stand shoulder to shoulder."

"It's my back I'm worried about," said the Chargé. "Come and see me some time. Come to dinner. Bring Zeinab."

"I will, tomorrow," Owen promised.

The Chargé waved a hand and turned back into the group. Paul drew Owen a little further away.

"That's another problem," said Owen.

"What?"

"Zeinab."

"Forget Zeinab. What are we going to do about this mess?"

"I can suppress it for a time. I can garble it when it comes out. I can camouflage it with other things. But in the end it will come out."

"How long's the end?"

"Two weeks, perhaps three. Two days if we're unlucky."

"The Agreement will take at least another month."

"Why don't we just disown Narouz? We and the Khedive?"

"It *is* Narouz, is it?"

"Well," Owen admitted, "we can't be completely certain."

"We can hardly disown him publicly, then."

"I wasn't thinking of going as far as that. I was just thinking that if the case were unblocked—"

"Gareth," said Paul, "are you absolutely certain that you didn't plant the story yourself?"

"Absolutely certain. I would have remembered a thing like that."

"It's just that it's amazingly convenient."

"It seems so, I know. But actually," said Owen, "I find it rather worrying. You see, up to now we've been able to keep it fairly tight. But this means it may be moving out of our control. Once people get hold of a thing like this they can start using it."

"So?"

"It needs to be wrapped up quickly. We want to get it out of the way before it starts escalating. Let Mahmoud get on with it. If it is Narouz, and the Khedive is bothered, we can tell Narouz to get out of the country quick. If it's not, we can finish it off without too many questions being asked. But we've got to move fast."

"This haste," said Paul, "it's not anything to do with Zeinab, is it?"

"Certainly not," said Owen.

⚬⚬⚬

Zeinab kissed him.

"I knew you would find a way," she said.

Owen kissed her back: then said, "Actually, it's not me."

Zeinab pushed him away. "What do you mean: it's not you?"

Owen reluctantly let her go.

"It's someone else. Nothing to do with me."

"I don't understand," said Zeinab.

"Someone else leaked it. Or else found it out. They gave it to *Al-Liwa*."

"It's not in *Al-Liwa*. I was reading it this morning."

"I know. I cut it out."

"You cut it out? Then...?"

"I just used it. Privately."

Zeinab couldn't make it out. However, she was prepared to give him the benefit of the doubt.

"Well," she said, "at least that's something."

"The effect is the same. The case is unblocked. Mahmoud can get on with it. So why don't we—"

"Not so fast," said Zeinab. "You haven't done anything yet."

"I've unblocked the case, haven't I?"

"I don't think that counts."

"Oh, come on—"

"No. That's not enough. I want Leila avenged."

"Avenged! Look, at the most all I could do was bring whoever did it to trial."

"As long as they die," said Zeinab, "I don't mind about the means."

"I can't do that!"

"If you can't," said Zeinab, "I won't."

And wouldn't be moved. Owen went off in a huff and read the papers. Zeinab curled up on a divan, deliberately provocatively, thought Owen, and ate Turkish Delight.

After a while Owen said: "There's something you could do to help."

"I might be prepared to do that," conceded Zeinab, dusting the powder from her fingers. "What did you have in mind?"

⚬⚬⚬

A call came from Prince Narouz.

"He's got the message quick," said Owen.

"He wants you to see him," said Nikos.

The Prince was waiting for him on the terrace of the Hotel Continental, sitting by himself and looking bored. His eyes lit up when he saw Owen.

"My dear fellow!" He waved him up. "A drink? Whisky, perhaps?"

He was having one himself. It was another of those things, like the green car, which made him a less than perfect Moslem. It would also, Owen thought, make him a less than perfect candidate for Khedive when a vacancy arose. Perhaps the British should back off him.

He sat down at the table and looked over the balustrade at the Street of the Camel below. It was the Regent Street of Cairo; except that in Regent Street you would not see a man walking by with a stuffed crocodile on his head or a pig being carried by in a cage.

What you would see, of course, were tourists and there were plenty of these. They came down the steps of the hotel with their Kodaks—at the Continental there was always a large number of Americans—and were immediately fallen upon by dragomans, donkey-boys and street traders of all kinds, all offering instant picturesqueness without the trouble of having to go too far in the heat to find it.

"Have you noticed," said the Prince, "that their business has changed? They used to sell beads and hippopotamus-hide whips and boa constrictors. Now they sell themselves to be photographed. That man, for instance"—he pointed to the one with the stuffed crocodile on his head—"he does not expect to actually sell the damned thing. Who would want to buy a stuffed crocodile? But a photograph, ah, well, that's a different thing. The tourist can carry it home much more conveniently; and the crocodile remains to be used another day."

The Prince sipped his whisky.

"From the point of view of trade it is an improvement. But to my mind it's got the thing the wrong way round. The really exotic thing is the camera. And for that"—he looked around with distaste—"you don't need to come to Egypt."

"There are, after all, other places."

"True; and I wish I were in them."

"Ah well, you may be able to escape soon," said Owen, saying the thing he thought he was being invited to say.

"You think so? Well, I hope you are right. This family business goes on and on."

The waiter brought Owen a whisky packed with ice, and a little pewter jug of water, also iced. Even in the best hotels they tended to view whisky as a kind of *pastis* and served it for drinking in the French way.

"And how, my dear fellow, are you getting on with your case?" asked the Prince.

"Oh," said Owen, "it moves, like all these things, in fits and starts. At the moment, I would say, it was starting again."

"Oh, good," said the Prince. He looked, however, troubled.

"Yes," said Owen, "I think it will soon be picking up momentum."

"Excellent," said the Prince, fidgeting with his glass.

"We'll soon be getting somewhere."

The Prince swirled the ice in the bottom of his glass and inspected it. He was about to speak and then thought better of it.

Owen smiled encouragingly and waited.

"I would like to help," said the Prince suddenly. "I have been thinking over your suggestion the other day. Perhaps I was too hasty in rejecting it."

"About the money?"

"Yes. I said then that it was a matter for the Government. But then, looking at it another way, I am, loosely speaking, the Government. In the old days, in a case like this, you would have appealed directly to the Khedive, not gone through layers of stupid bureaucracy. You were absolutely right to come direct to me. Right and proper."

"Ye—es?"

This was not quite what Owen had expected.

"And it was wrong of me to reject it out of hand. I was not being true," said the Prince, looking at him earnestly, "to my responsibilities."

"No?" said Owen, a little taken aback.

"No. You see, I was relieved. I thought it might all be going to go away without me having to do anything. That it might all blow over without any unpleasantness—"

"Unpleasantness?"

"Publicity."

"Oh yes. Of course."

"A woman dead." The Prince waved a hand. "Sad. But what's a woman dead in Egypt?"

"Quite."

"So," said the Prince, "I thought I would let it all blow over."

"Mm." Owen sounded disapproving.

"You're right. It wouldn't do. I couldn't do it. Not when it came to it. Well, it's not too late to put things right."

"Put things right?"

"You can have the money, my dear fellow. Count on me."

Owen was dumbfounded. What was this? He had been half expecting a confession. Not an offer of help!

Wait a minute: was this quite what it seemed? Was it a genuine offer? Or did the Prince expect something in return?

"I am most grateful, Your Highness," he said cautiously. "Indeed, I am overwhelmed. But, um, the money will go to redeeming the body, you know."

"Of course," said the Prince, surprised. "What else? Oh, I see. Well, no. Not this time."

"In that case I can only express my gratitude. I will get in touch with Mr. el Zaki immediately."

The Prince regarded him thoughtfully.

"I know what you think," he said suddenly. "You think I did it. Killed the girl. Well, I didn't. Indeed not."

☙

"I'm not sure that we need his money," said Mahmoud.

"Well, ordinarily I wouldn't pay that sort of price—"

"I think we can do without it."

Mahmoud, Owen knew, did not like paying money for information. It smacked too much of the Old Egypt of bribes and favors which he wanted to sweep away. Trained in the French school of severe deductive logic, he preferred to rely on unassisted reason. Assemble your knowledge and analyze it: that was the way forward. Not haphazard reliance on rumor and gossip.

He was different from Owen. Owen purchased information every day. He had his agents out in the bazaars and souks and offered a steady price for good information. He had inherited when he became Mamur Zapt a vast network of spies, informers and paid agents which dated back to his Ottoman predecessors and which the British saw no reason to disturb.

It was the difference between a detective and an Intelligence Officer. Even in India, where Owen had served before he came to Egypt, and where in his latter years he had been seconded from his regiment to an Intelligence post on the Frontier, it had been normal practice to purchase information. He found Mahmoud curiously puritanical.

"The fact is," said Mahmoud, "I don't think we need it."

"How else are we going to find the body now that those buggers have pinched it?" demanded Owen.

Mahmoud frowned. Owen thought for a moment that he was taking exception to the casual obscenity, but it was not that. He was bothered by "pinch." Mahmoud's knowledge of English, as of French, was superb but army colloquial occasionally threw him.

"Stolen," Owen amended.

"Ah yes, 'pinch,'" murmured Mahmoud, filing the word away for future reference. "Well," he said, "I think I have found out who did—pinch?—it."

"You've found the body?" said Owen incredulously.

"No, not yet," Mahmoud admitted. "But I have, I think, found the men. And that is where, my friend"—he placed his arm affectionately round Owen in the Arab way—"I need your help. For I do not think they will talk to me, not without encouragement. The Parquet, you see, is something new to them and the police they view with derision."

"New?" said Owen. The Parquet had existed, he thought, since at least 1883 when a reforming Minister of Justice had unearthed in his office some Arabic translations of parts of the French Code Napoléon and promulgated them as the new Egyptian legal system.

"New to them," said Mahmoud, urging Owen toward an arabeah drawn up beside the pavement. "Whereas the Mamur Zapt," he said, as they settled back into the shabby, hot leather, "is old. They are used to him. And they know," said Mahmoud, smiling, "that he is even more merciless than— well, wait and see."

"Look," said Owen, "I'm not—"

"All you have to do is just sit there," Mahmoud reassured him. "The name will be enough."

"Who are these people?"

༄

They were, Mahmoud explained, the beggars who normally worked the part of the river where Leila's body had come ashore.

"They all have their territory," said Mahmoud. "It was just a case of finding who they were."

That had not been difficult since they were, in fact, known to all the neighborhood. The boatmen knew them, the watchman knew them—he greeted them every day—and the police certainly knew them.

Mahmoud had had, however, some good fortune. He had remembered having seen, that first day, some goats grazing further on down the riverbank, had made some inquiries and discovered that they were taken down on to the riverbed every morning by a boy who acted as herd.

He had found the boy and questioned him. Yes, he had taken the goats down that particular morning. No, he had not seen a body, still less a woman's body. If he had, he might have gone out and had a look.

But he did remember seeing the two beggars. Their names were Farag and Libab and he saw them every day. They worked the bank where his goats grazed and they would always stop and have a chat.

He remembered that day because Farag had asked him if he had a sister. He did have a sister but he thought that, poor though his family was, it would not be very keen on her marrying a beggar. Where was the profit in that?

He had pointed that out to Farag but Farag had not been put off. He had said that things might be going to change. The boy had scoffed at this but Farag had told him to wait and see. He was still waiting.

It would have been, he said, late in the morning when the men were coming back. They worked outward from the city to a point not far south of the Souk al-Gadira and then returned, thus making two sweeps of the riverbank. They made caches on their way out which they picked up as they returned.

"What do they make caches of?" asked Owen.

"Wood, mostly."

Wood was in short supply in the city. It was the main fuel used for large-scale cooking and faggots were brought into the city every day. It had to come from some distance away since over the centuries the trees and bushes on both sides of the river had been lopped down. Driftwood, then, fetched a not inconsiderable price.

So there was evidence that the beggars had been on the bank that morning. And there was the additional point that on their return they had appeared cheerful, as if from a windfall.

ᠥᠠᠠᠥ

They were being held at the local police station. The Chief had resigned himself to Mahmoud but had not been expecting Owen. When he saw him he flinched slightly. His doom still hung over him like a sword.

The two beggars were crouched in the courtyard. One affected to be lame and had probably become so by constant practice. The other affected blindness and certainly had something wrong with his eyes, though half the population of Egypt suffered from ophthalmia and the eyes couldn't have been too bad since he relied on them every day.

Mahmoud, sitting behind the Chief's desk to better express the awful power of the state, had them brought in.

Owen sat behind the two men, back in a corner. They did not see him as they came in.

"You are Farag," said Mahmoud, "and you are Libab?"

"Yes, effendi."

"And you patrol the bank every day and what you find you take back to the Man?"

The beggars hesitated.

"We patrol the bank, yes."

It was best not to use the name of the Man.

Mahmoud had established, though, that he knew him.

"Think back," said Mahmoud, "think back to the morning when you asked the boy Farakat about his sister. What had happened that morning to make you think, Farag, that you were rich enough to afford a wife?"

"It was idle talk," said Farag. "I do not remember."

"I think you do remember," said Mahmoud, "but you do not want to tell me. And that is foolish. Foolish because I may know the answer already and just be testing you. Foolish because if you do not tell me, I have the power to take you away from the riverbank, away from the sun and light, and shut you in the caracol forever."

"At least it would be cool there," said Farag sturdily.

"And they would give us food," said Libab.

"Every day," said Farag. "I have heard."

The whole population had heard. An unexpected side effect of Cromer's reform of the prison system was to make conditions inside prison better for the poor than they often were outside.

"Forever," repeated Mahmoud, significantly but untruthfully. That was another change. In the old days a man could be left to languish in prison uncharged and forgotten. Nowadays his case had to be heard within a given time.

The beggars were not impressed. They felt they might be onto a good thing. Indeed, the more they reflected on it, the better it appeared, and they quickly passed from affecting forgetfulness to unaffected obduracy. There had been nothing out of the ordinary about that morning, they said, nothing.

"You did not find something on the riverbank that you thought had made your fortune?"

"That would have just been a dream," said Libab.

"Yet you, Farag, believed the dream was real enough for you to fancy you were rich," Mahmoud pointed out.

"That was mere fancy," said Farag.

Mahmoud could not break through. He sat silent for a moment, thinking.

The beggars, emboldened, became cheeky.

"You can't do anything to us," said Libab. "Let us go!"

"What if we did find something on the bank?" asked Farag. "What is that to you?"

"Little to me," Mahmoud admitted. He had made up his mind how to play the next bit now. "But a lot to the Mamur Zapt."

"The Mamur Zapt? What's he got to do with it?"

"You're just dragging him in," said Farag. "The Mamur Zapt is not interested in the likes of us."

"On the contrary," said Owen from behind them. "I find you very interesting."

The men froze.

Mahmoud came round the desk and sat on the front of it. "There you are," he said amiably. "What did I tell you?"

Farag tried to look over his shoulder. Mahmoud reached forward, took him by the head and turned his face back towards him.

"You are talking to me. Would you like me to take them through it?" he asked Owen over their shoulders.

"Please do."

"Well, then. Let us begin with what you found on the riverbank."

"We found nothing on the riverbank," said Farag, still sturdily but less confidently.

"The girl's body. As you came along the bank, where was it lying?"

"We saw no girl's body."

"On the shoal. A little out from the bank. As I said, perhaps I know the answers already. Tell me what you did when you saw the body."

"We saw no—" began Farag, and stopped.

"The Mamur Zapt is beginning to get impatient," said Mahmoud. "And I don't think I will help you anymore."

"We saw the body," whispered Libab. "And I said to Farag, 'There it is.'"

"So!" Mahmoud nodded approvingly. He turned to Farag. "And what did you say?"

"I said," replied Farag reluctantly, "I said: 'Perhaps it is not. Perhaps it is another. Let us go and see.'"

"So you walked out to the shoal and—?"

"We saw that it was the body."

"How did you know that it was the right body?"

"By the dress," whispered Libab.

"The shintiyan?"

He caught their look of surprise.

"As I told you. I know everything. They were pink, I think?"

"Yes, effendi."

Libab, at any rate, was docile now.

"It wasn't just the shintiyan," said Farag, caving into line.

"Oh? What was it?"

"It wasn't a peasant woman, you see. Most of the ones that come down are."

"You knew she wouldn't be?"

"That's right."

"You had been told?"

"Yes."

"Who by?"

Farag hesitated. "You know," he muttered.

"The Man?"

Libab looked involuntarily over his shoulder, half saw Owen and was transfixed.

"Yes," said Mahmoud chattily. "It is difficult, isn't it? The Mamur Zapt stands on one side of you, the Man on the other. I would watch my step if I were you. So you had found what you had been told to find. What then?"

"Well," said Farag, "we saw the ghaffir coming. So we ran away and hid."

"We thought he might not see the body," said Libab.

"But he did. He went down on to the bank and looked at it. And then he looked around to find someone he could send to the omda. But there was no one."

"We stayed hid."

"He had to go himself."

"Then Farag said to me: 'Let us take the body now, before he comes back.' So we ran into the water and took the body."

"What did you do with the body?"

"Carried it behind the wall."

"It was as far as we could get," explained Farag, "because then the ghaffir came back."

"But first the policeman came with his pole. That was good, wasn't it?"

"He didn't know what to make of it."

"We laughed. Farag laughed so loudly I thought they would hear us."

"Because then the ghaffir came back and he was even more amazed."

"And then the Englishman came down—"

"And that was a good laugh too, I expect," said Owen.

"Yes, it was," said Libab enthusiastically. "There they were, all three of them, scratching their heads and wondering where the body was—"

"And all the time it was behind the wall. Right nearby!"

"Very funny," said Mahmoud. "And how long did it stay behind the wall?"

"Until they were all gone. A lot of people came down. You were there yourself, weren't you?"

"Yes," said Mahmoud. "I was."

The merriment died away.

"Well, yes," said Farag.

"Yes," echoed Libab faintly.

"Yes. So what did you do then? With the body?"

"We hid it."

"Where?"

"Under a boat. There's a boatman along the bank. He does things for the Man sometimes. We went to him and said: 'We have hidden something for the Man under one of your boats.' And the boatman said: 'Tell me which boat it is so that I will know which boat not to look under.' And we told him. And he said: 'I will see that it stays there until the Man sends someone for it.'"

"Show me the boat," said Mahmoud.

They showed him the boat. But when he lifted the
upturned boat and peered into the hollow beneath it he found
nothing there.

Chapter 8

"So the Man has it," said Owen.

They were walking home along the riverbank. The sudden, brief Egyptian twilight had come upon them while they were looking at the boat. One moment the sun had been hanging above the desert, the next it had plunged out of sight, leaving only the copper and rose and saffron of the water to testify that it had been there.

As the shadows closed over the land the heat went out of the day. A delicate river breeze sprang up. Mahmoud and Owen looked at each other, then with one accord started walking.

The beggars had been sent to the caracol. All the information they possessed had probably been got out of them, but if they were released they would simply disappear. They might even, as Mahmoud pointed out, disappear for good.

"More than that," said Mahmoud. "He not only has it but he sent them to fetch it."

"So he knew it would be there."

"And that," said Mahmoud, "takes us back to what happened on the dahabeeyah that night."

"And rules out one thing: that she fell overboard by accident."

"Or jumped of her own accord."

"He knew the body would be there. He knew it beforehand. Which makes it—"

"Yes," said Mahmoud, "I would think so."

As darkness fell, the birds began their evensong. There were not many trees in the poorer part of the city but the few trees there were, preserved to give shade in the little squares, were full of birds. From the topmost branches where the pigeons sat came a continuous cooing.

"He must have had somebody on the boat," said Owen.

"It looks like it."

"Who killed her and threw the body overboard."

"Don't we have difficulties there?" asked Mahmoud. "Surely if it was thrown overboard there was no guarantee that it would finish up on shore where the Man could send someone to fetch it. It could just as easily have gone on to Bulak bridge. Or beyond, for that matter."

"How far offshore was the dahabeeyah?"

"Not far. It was moored for the night."

"Could the body have been dumped straight onto the shoal?"

"They would have had to have taken it ashore."

"A rowing boat, perhaps?"

"Surely someone on board would have seen it?"

"Perhaps they were looking the other way."

"Deliberately, you mean?"

"Yes."

"They might have been told to."

"Yes."

"Well," said Owen thoughtfully, "it would figure. The body was high up on the shoal, wasn't it? We wondered how it had got there. We thought it might be a bow wave from a steamer."

"So we did. Yes," said Mahmoud, "that would figure."

෬᎗᎗᎗෨

"So we're going to have to deal," concluded Owen.

Garvin looked dubious.

"It's pretty definite that he's got the body. And if we want it, that's what we've got to pay."

"*Do* we want the body?" asked Garvin. "That much?"

"How else are we going to find out how she was killed?"

"It's a lot of money."

"It would need a supplementary allocation. I'm over the top on that budget as it is."

Garvin pursed his lips.

"I put in for a supplementary allocation only last week," he said. "They'll say, 'What, another?'"

"Well, I can't see any other way of doing it."

"I can just see them," said Garvin, "when I go along. 'Please can I have a supplementary allocation.' 'What, another?' 'Yes, it's to buy a body, you see.' It would look bad on paper, Owen. These accounts go back to London. There are MPs who crawl over everything we do. They'd spot it and say, 'What the hell is this?' They'd think it was the Mahdi's skull all over again."

The Mahdi's skull had been a *cause célèbre*. At the conclusion of the Sudan wars, shortly before, the victorious British general, Kitchener, had smashed the tomb of the defeated enemy and claimed his skull as a souvenir. It had been alleged in London, possibly truthfully, that he had intended to make a drinking tankard of it.

"Well, how else am I going to find the money? Narouz has said he'll help but in the circumstances—"

Garvin looked at him quickly.

"Yes," he said. "In the circumstances. You really think—?"

"Well," said Owen, "it looks like it."

"I don't like it," said Garvin. "This is going to look bad. It could be very awkward. We don't want it turning up just when—"

"We're not there yet," said Owen defensively.

"Suppose it comes up just when we're about to sign the Agreement? It could blow the whole thing. You're supposed to be keeping it under control, Owen. What the hell are you doing?"

"Look, I'm not—" Owen began but decided it was a waste of time. "What about this money?" he asked.

"Don't like it," said Garvin. "It would look bad in the Accounts. 'Item: one body. Purchased for the Mamur Zapt. Private use of.' No," said Garvin, shaking his head, "it wouldn't look good at all. I really don't think I could support a bid for a supplementary allocation. Not in the circumstances."

ᏇᎷᏋ

"I'm afraid not," said Prince Narouz, shaking his head regretfully. "Not in the circumstances."

"But only two days ago—"

"Circumstances have changed."

"In two days?"

"Things are very fluid just at the moment."

They were sitting again on the terrace at the Continental. The sun was still bright and the Prince was wearing huge, dark green sunglasses. The tables were filling up for afternoon tea. A party of French tourists arrived from the bazaars and made their way up the steps. One of them was a strikingly beautiful woman in her mid-thirties. The dark green glasses followed her progress indoors.

"Why have they changed?"

"Oh, well," said the Prince vaguely. "You know."

"The Agreement?"

"That, too."

"It's near signing?"

"*They* think so," said the Prince caustically. "Personally, I don't believe my uncle will be able to bring himself to do it when the moment actually comes. The prospect of having the British here for another twenty years! Frightful!"

The Prince looked at Owen, laughed archly and placed a placating hand on Owen's.

"Or so my uncle will think. Of course, I myself see it differently. I would be only too delighted if the British were to remain."

And had, no doubt, been communicating that fact very successfully, thought Owen bitterly.

"A breath of Western air, my dear fellow," said the Prince. "That's what Egypt needs. Cars, bridges, roads, factories: we need to step through into the modern age."

With plenty of contracts for British firms. The Prince, thought Owen, knew how to play his hand.

"So you have changed your mind," he said.

"Oh, I wouldn't say that!" the Prince protested. "No, no, my dear fellow, I am still eager to help. You can count on me, believe me. But things are—delicate, just at the moment. Let's not rush. More haste, less speed. Although"—the Prince turned reflective—"speaking as a driver, that is a phrase I have always found puzzling."

"The offer might not remain open."

"You think so?" The Prince looked at him thoughtfully. "You think so?"

"There might be others."

The Prince turned it over. Turned it over thoughtfully.

"I can see there is a risk. However"—he smiled charmingly—"it is a risk I am prepared to run."

"So you won't help after all?"

"I'm afraid not. Not just now. Not in the circumstances."

Owen could see it all. The Prince, once again, had scented the possibility of wriggling off the hook. The British had refused to buy the body. Why should he stick his own neck into the noose? If he didn't find the money, perhaps no one would find the money. The body would remain where it was. What did it matter if there was a leak in the Press? They wouldn't be able to prove anything. Why not just leave things alone?

And meanwhile cast a little bread upon the waters. A hint here, a hint there. A suggestion that the Khedive was not perhaps entirely dependable. A reminder of his own Western sympathies. An intimation of trade concessions, contracts for British firms.

No wonder, thought Owen bitterly, that Garvin had backed off.

There would be no deal with the Man; that was plain.

Unless—

Owen stopped in his tracks.

Unless Narouz made one of his own.

ᏮᏇᎧᎧᎩ

Owen sat cursing himself. What folly! What utter folly! To go to the one man in the world most interested in seeing that the evidence never came out and then to put into his hands the means of ensuring that it never could come out! How had he come to do a thing like that?

He knew what had put the idea in his head. It had been that first visit to the police station, when the Prince had dangled money in front of the local chief. He had been prepared to put his money down then. Why not, Owen had thought, get him to put his money down later, when it could really do some good?

When he had gone to him, the Prince had in fact at first turned the suggestion down. It hadn't really bothered Owen; it had just been something to try.

But then when Narouz had himself raised it and indicated that he had changed his mind, it had suddenly come to seem a good idea.

Perhaps Narouz had even then been playing a game with him. Perhaps even then he had no real intention of finding the money for the body, or at least not of presenting Owen with it.

But, looking back on the conversation, Owen did not think so. The offer had seemed genuine. Something had been troubling Narouz. It might simply have been the fear of publicity. Owen had a feeling, though, that it was something else. Narouz had spoken of family worries.

Whatever it was, Narouz had switched again. But this time there was a difference. He now knew almost for certain that the British were not prepared to find the money. That meant the way was now open for him to strike a private deal.

And he, Owen, had given him the information! What a fool! What an idiot!

What could he do now? Nothing, as far as he could see. Narouz had the information. All he had to do was strike a bargain. And once he'd got the body, that was that. He would dispose of it and a key item of evidence would be gone for good.

It was all very well Mahmoud saying they didn't need the body. In theory that might be true. If the other evidence was good enough they could secure a conviction on that alone.

But could they ever secure a conviction on that basis against an heir to the throne? He would be defended not just by the best lawyers in Egypt but probably by the best lawyers in France. The case would have to be watertight. And without incontrovertible evidence that Leila was dead, would it ever be watertight enough?

It wouldn't even get to prosecution. The whole weight of the State would be ganged up against it. The Khedive, the Minister of Justice, the Parquet, the British—the British would be against it, too, particularly if this damned Agreement was still on the cards. It wouldn't have a chance, in the circumstances, of even reaching the courts.

In the circumstances. That was what they had both said. Both Garvin and Narouz. Now he was saying the same thing. It was what anyone would say, anyone used to politics or business or the world of affairs generally. When you had been in that world for a while you knew the way things would go. So?

What was he saying? Was he saying that when you knew the way things would go, you went along with them? Wasn't that being defeatist?

Well, no, not really. It was being sensible; it was being realistic. If you were involved in things at a senior level, whether it were as an administrator, a Minister or even as a senior policeman, you had hundreds of things on the go at any one time. And if you knew that pushing one particular thing was going to get you nowhere you didn't waste time going on pushing it; you left off and started pushing something else. That way you got *something* done, at any rate.

So did that mean he ought to forget about Leila? That was what Garvin was more or less saying; that was what, he suspected, Paul would say.

What it boiled down to was a question of priorities. A set of priorities went with the job and if you took on the job you took on the priorities. His priorities were pretty plain. The Mamur Zapt was in charge of law and order in Cairo and that meant keeping the city quiet and stopping them all from getting at each other's throats. And in the circumstances that was pretty difficult and—

In the circumstances. There he was again.

Zeinab had said something about that. She had said he was too much a man of circumstances, that when the circumstances changed, he changed.

Well, she would say that, wouldn't she? It was easier for a woman. A woman's world was more private, she was in charge of it in a way that you couldn't be if you were a man. In a man's world you were forever running up against things. Yes, you were more interested by circumstances. They kept bloody coming up and hitting you in the face.

He couldn't ignore circumstances. They were part of his world; they *were* his world. And he liked his world, damn it!

So what was he going to do about Leila? If anything.

ᏇᎲᎲᎧ

Zeinab announced that she was taking Owen to the theater.

"Not another *New Roses*, is it?" asked Owen suspiciously.

"It *is* by Gamal, as it happens," said Zeinab haughtily. "At least, the translation is by him. The original play is by an Englishman, though what Gamal is doing translating plays by Englishmen I cannot think. It is called *Love's Labour's Lost*."

"*Love's Labour's Lost*? But that's by Shakespeare."

"I don't know anything about that," said Zeinab. "But I thought from the title that it might have something special to say to you. That is not the only reason why we are going, however."

"No?"

"You remember you asked me to see if I could find out who it was that had sent the news item about Leila in to *Al-Liwa*."

"If you could do it discreetly, yes."

"Naturally. Well, I talked to Gamal's journalist friends. Most of them work on the arts pages and don't know much about the rest of the paper. But one of them is a copy editor, I think that is what he is called, and he told me that he thought the item had come in from a friend of Leila's."

"Did he know his name?"

"He wasn't sure. He thought he had seen him, though, at Gamal's soirées. He had usually been with a girl, an Arab girl, which was unusual, of course, and had made him stand out."

"Leila?"

"Probably. Anyway, he saw him again in the office at *Al-Liwa* just before the item appeared. Or would have appeared if you had not crossed it out. So he thinks perhaps it came from him."

"Could he check?"

"No. He says you don't check things like that at a radical paper like *Al-Liwa*."

"Fair enough. It would be useful to have the bloke's name, that's all."

"Well—" said Zeinab, looking smug.

"Well, what?"

"I had an idea. Do you remember that when we were talking to Gamal and his friends they mentioned some of the men that Leila had gone around with?"

"Suleiman."

"And others. Well, one of them—you remember?—was a journalist."

"So he was. But I don't remember—"

"Hargazy. That was his name. Anyway, I checked. And—" Zeinab paused dramatically.

"Yes?"

"He works for *Al-Liwa*."

"Does he now? Does he now?"

"Yes," said Zeinab, pleased with the effect. "Not all the time. He is not on their permanent staff—they don't have many permanent staff, of course, because you put them in prison—"

"No, I don't. *Al-Liwa* doesn't make any money; that's why they don't have many permanent staff."

"Anyway. Hargazy just does the occasional article for them. He covers demonstrations, that sort of thing, Gamal's friend said."

"I'll take a look at him."

"*We'll* take a look at him. That is why we are going to the theater. I've asked Gamal to invite him specially. And, just to be sure, I've asked Gamal's friend, the one who works in *Al-Liwa*, to be there too."

"My God!" said Owen. "Anything else?"

"Not at the moment," said Zeinab.

Owen kissed her. That much, at least, she allowed.

ᴼᵐᵐᴼ

The Arab Theater was a barnlike building which on its better days could seat an audience of two hundred. This was not one of its better days. The Arab predilection for drama, at least in personal relationships, did not extend to a taste for Shakespeare's comedies translated into Arabic, and the house was less than half full.

The first three rows, seated in rather tatty red plush armchairs, were occupied by Gamal's friends and supporters and were respectable, at least in terms of numbers. It was on the wooden benches behind that the gaps appeared. They were, in fact, mostly gap.

Behind them was a row of flimsily partitioned wooden boxes. Half of them, the ones with wooden grilles, were for the women. The others were for the nass taibin, the really well-to-do.

This presented a problem for Zeinab, who was quite definitely a woman but didn't like to sit invisible and fenced off from her friends. She was, however, also well-to-do, so she compromised by sitting in the open box next to the screened harem ones.

She was, though, the only woman doing this and attracted pointings-out and mutterings, not to say ribaldry. She had made a gesture in the direction of decency by wearing a veil, behind which she sat disdainfully. She was, nevertheless, not entirely comfortable.

Gamal and one or two of his friends had joined them in the box and Gamal was not entirely comfortable either, though for different reasons.

"They are not laughing," he said. "This is terrible!"

"They are enjoying it quietly," said Owen soothingly.

"Yes, but—are they not seeing the jokes? Haven't I brought them out sufficiently?"

"It's not always easy to get the jokes. Even in the English."

"I should have brought them out more."

"That's not so easy. So many of them are based on word-play, puns."

"But you see, that's why I chose the play. Arabic has a tradition of wordplay, too. I thought I would bring out the affinity between Elizabethan English and classical Arabic."

"You have," Owen assured him, "you have!"

Zeinab followed the play with interest.

"I like that bit," she said. "When she sends him away to make jokes in a hospital. 'To move wild laughter in the throat of death.' Yes, I like that."

"I agree with him," said Owen. "Twelve months is too long."

"What I *don't* like," said Zeinab, "is having men play the women's parts."

"You have to do that," said Gamal. "It's unseemly to have women onstage."

"I've seen women onstage here," Owen objected.

"Ah yes. Foreign women. And sometimes we have Jews. But not Arab women; that wouldn't be right."

"It's not right to have boys," said Zeinab, "not when it's a question of making love."

"It's not *making* love," said Gamal. "It's talking love."

"There's something to be said for that," said Zeinab, with a sidelong glance at Owen.

"In England in Shakespeare's time," said Owen, disregarding her, "the women's parts would probably have been played by boys."

"I am against confusion on a matter like this," said Zeinab.

Fortunately, some of Gamal's friends burst into the box at this point.

"Brilliant, Gamal! Exquisite!"

"The wit!"

"You think so?" said Gamal, pleased. "I was worried—"

They bore him off to their favorite café.

Owen and Zeinab tailed along. Zeinab was talking to a tall, thin youth who seemed rather overwhelmed by her presence.

"You're sure?" she said.

"Yes," said the youth, shyly but firmly.

Zeinab dropped back alongside Owen.

"This is Hafiz. He works on *Al-Liwa*."

"A paper I always read," said Owen truthfully.

"Really?" said the young man, gratified. "I've only just started there. They don't let me do much yet. Copyediting, that sort of thing."

"They have a very small staff. You've done extraordinarily well to get onto it at all."

"Well," said the young man modestly, "I suppose I had quite a reputation. I used to edit a radical student newspaper. *Sword of Islam*. I don't suppose…?"

"Oh yes," said Owen, again truthfully. "I have read it."

He read all the radical papers.

"Excellent," he assured the young man. "I am sure you have a considerable career ahead of you."

"I was asking Hafiz," said Zeinab, "if Hargazy was the one who came to the office."

"Which is Hargazy?"

Zeinab pointed out a balding man in an open-necked red shirt.

"And was he?"

"Yes," said Hafiz.

When they reached the café, Zeinab drew up a chair beside Hargazy.

He responded to her at once. Most people did.

"I don't think we've met?"

"Although I've certainly seen you," said Zeinab. "You must be one of the few friends of Gamal that I don't know."

"I know Feisal better than I know Gamal. He brings me along," said Hargazy, smiling, "to occasions like this."

They talked about the play.

"You obviously know a lot about writing," said Zeinab.

"I should," said Hargazy. "That's how I earn my living."

"Really? A playwright? Or perhaps a novelist?"

"Not yet," admitted Hargazy, a trifle grudgingly. "I've got one or two things coming along. Rather good things, actually. But at the moment I'm still freelancing."

He told her he contributed to *Al-Liwa*.

"That's a real paper," said Zeinab enthusiastically. "I wish I could work for it."

"Well," said Hargazy, laughing, "I'm afraid that's out of the question. A woman, after all—"

"Women do write," said Zeinab. "In France they write."

"Ah, in France." Hargazy shrugged his shoulders.

"I *have* seen you before," said Zeinab. "And wasn't it with a girl? An Arab girl? I remember, because it was so unusual. What was her name?"

"Leila." He looked at her a little warily.

"That's right. How is she? Or shouldn't I ask?"

The man didn't reply. He looked down at the ground.

"I'm sorry," said Zeinab. "Perhaps you've split up?"

"No," said Hargazy, "no."

"She looked an interesting girl. I had a sort of fellow feeling for her."

"Really?" Hargazy looked at her sharply. "Why should you have a fellow feeling for her?"

Now it was Zeinab who shrugged.

"I don't know," she said. "Nothing, really. It was just that she was another Egyptian girl. Among so many foreign ones."

"That was it," said Hargazy. "That was what made her stand out."

"I shouldn't ask about her," said Zeinab. "I'm sorry."

"No, not at all. It's good to ask about her."

"No, it's not," said Zeinab. "I remember now: She is dead."

"Yes," said the man, "she is dead." He looked down at the ground, then looked up. "They killed her," he said.

"'They'?"

"The ones who kill us every day."

"I don't understand," said Zeinab.

"You must understand," said the man. He waved an arm excitedly. "The ones who hold us down. Stamp on us. Destroy what is best of Egypt."

"The British?"

"They are just the tools," said Hargazy contemptuously. "If it wasn't them it would be the Turks. Or the French. No, it's the ones who bring them in, who brought them in in the first place—"

"The Khedive?"

"And the rich. The whole pack of them. They are like a great yoke sitting on our shoulders. They weight us down, they rob us, they starve us. They beat us—"

His shoulders heaved.

"They beat me," he said in a strangled voice. "When I was a boy. The Pasha's overseer struck my father. I said: 'Do not do that.' He said, 'I will teach you to talk to me like that.' And then he beat me, and my father watched—and did nothing!"

His voice choked.

"It was then I realized: he could do nothing. Nothing, while all those people were in place. Nothing, while they were the ones who held the curbash."

Zeinab, that daughter of a Pasha and representative of the rich, sat silent.

"They kill us," said the man bitterly. "And they killed Leila."

"If they killed Leila," said Zeinab, "then that should be made known."

The man looked at her sharply and seemed about to speak. Then he thought better of it.

"Yes," he said. "Yes."

"If you need help," said Zeinab, "call on me."

⌘

There was, said Nikos, a deputation waiting to see him.

"Show them in," instructed Owen.

"I can't. They won't fit in."

"How many of them are there?"

"Sixty," said Nikos. "So far."

Owen had been conscious for some time of growing movement in the courtyard below. He went to the window and pushed open the shutters. The courtyard was full.

"I revise my estimate," said Nikos. "Eighty."

"What do they want?"

"It's something to do with bodies," said Nikos.

Owen went down into the courtyard. A little group of men were standing by the door waiting for him. Their faces seemed half familiar.

Georgiades suddenly appeared beside him.

"Marwash," he said, indicating one of the half-familiar faces. "He's the father of the girl."

"Girl?"

"The one whose tomb they used to put the arms in."

"Oh yes."

He recognized some of the faces now. There was the village omda and there was the local sheikh. And there was the fiki who had gone to the tomb with the women to chant the readings.

Georgiades, for some reason, was looking at him closely.

"Haven't I seen you before?" he said.

"You saw me at the tomb," replied the man.

"Somewhere else too."

The sheikh came towards Owen. He was a religious sheikh and presided at the mosque the girl's father attended.

They exchanged the prescribed greetings.

"A sad business," said Owen. "My heart goes out to the father and to all the family. Those responsible will be caught and punished."

It was a serious matter to profane a tomb. Apart from the distress it caused, there was the affront to religious suscepti-bilities. The authorities were always prompt to support the Mufti and the religious sheikhs on a thing like this. It could so easily spill over into civil disorder and violence.

"So they should be," said the sheikh. "Ali Marwash is greatly respected. However, that is not the reason why I have come to see you."

"No?"

Owen looked round. The courtyard was now overflowing with serious-faced, white-galabeahed men. There were others outside the gates. Outside the gates, too, he could see some respectably dressed women. It was unusual for women to appear at such a public occasion.

Policemen, armed, filed out of the building and took up position. He signed to them to keep back.

"Your troubles are my troubles," he said to the sheikh. "What can I do to help you?"

"It is the girl's body," said the sheikh.

"That it should be disturbed in this way is most regrettable."

"It is not there."

"Not there?" said Owen, dumbfounded.

"It is not in the tomb."

Surely his men had not removed the body with the guns?

"When we looked, it was not there."

"How can this be?"

"I don't know," said the sheikh, "but these are evil times."

"Has search been made?"

"Where should search be made?"

Perhaps the arms runners had removed the body, finding there was not enough room for the arms. But then, where would they have put it?

"The Place of Tombs," said Owen. "Perhaps it has been cast aside."

"We have looked," said the sheikh, "but we could not find it. And so we have come to you."

"It is wrong," said one of the men beside him, "wrong to trouble the dead."

There was a murmur of assent from the crowd.

"Cannot a body be left to rest in peace?" asked someone else.

The mutter grew louder. Beyond the gates a woman began to ululate.

"Who can have done this evil thing?"

"Not one of us," someone shouted from the back of the crowd.

"No," the fiki called back, "it was some unbeliever, I'll be bound!"

"Shut up!" snapped Owen.

"Shut up!" said Georgiades, pressing the fiki back against the wall. He peered in the man's face. "Haven't I seen you before?"

There were shouts now from all sides. Some men at the back of the crowd tried to force their way forward. The crowd surged alarmingly. The policemen fingered their rifles.

"Enough!"

Owen stepped forward and held up his hand.

"Enough! This wrong will be righted. But that is for the Mamur Zapt and not for you. Go back to the Place of Tombs. My men will come with you. We will search together until the body is found and restored to its rightful place."

This was well received but no one actually moved. Owen pushed his way into the crowd.

"I will lead you!" he shouted.

The crowd opened up and he headed for the gate. The sheikh fell in behind him.

"To the Place of Tombs!" shouted Georgiades, thrusting with his shoulders. The constables joined in enthusiastically. Gradually the crowd began to move.

Outside the gates they fell into a more or less orderly procession, Owen at their head. When they got to the Place of Tombs he would find a way of breaking them up. If they could find the body, that would be fine. He would assure them that the perpetrators would be punished and they would all go home happily.

It should not be too difficult to find the body. It must have been dumped somewhere nearby.

When he looked in the tomb he had not really noticed the body was missing. He had seen the arms and thought that was that. He had presumed the body was somewhere in the background.

God! Another body going missing! He'd thought for a moment that the fates had it in for him. But this, surely, was straightforward.

He hoped.

Chapter 9

At this time of day, late in the morning, there was no shade in the Place of Tombs for anyone, apart from those underground. The sun shone down with a bright, hard glare and was reflected off the stonework of the tombs. In the space between the tombs the heat was in the 130's.

This helped proceedings enormously. The crowd, which had at first congregated expectantly round the tomb, evidently hoping that the Mamur Zapt would conjure the girl, Lazarus-like, from the dead, wilted as the miracle continued to be deferred.

Weaker spirits spread out quickly in search not so much of the body as of shade. With the sun now almost directly overhead, the shadows cast by the tombs were thin and soon crowded. Stronger, or possibly more curious, spirits who deferred dispersal were obliged to seek further out. Thus in a short time the crowd dwindled to manageable proportions.

Georgiades, eager as always to get somebody else to do the work, organized those who remained into little groups which began to explore the area systematically. This thinned the crowd even further.

Where there was space to move, Owen set the constables to work. He expected to find the girl's body dumped unceremoniously in some gap between the tombs, not very far away, perhaps tucked under some slanting tombstone. The arms runners would not, he thought, have gone far out of their way to dispose of it.

The sheikh and the girl's father looked at him expectantly. They obviously hoped for more.

Owen couldn't think for the moment what more there was to be done, so he climbed up on an old ruined tombstone to survey the scene.

The Place of Tombs was a vast necropolis which over the centuries had spread until it occupied the space virtually to the horizon, where the light quavered in continuing mirages. You could date the different parts of the cemetery not just by the state of disrepair or ruination of the tombs but also by their style: the tombs of the Mamelukes often had cupolas raised over them painted blue and with golden lettering.

Here, where Ali Marwash's family were buried, and where he hoped to be buried himself—he had already purchased the ground and designed the tomb—were humbler brick tombs decorated only by upright headstones with turbans carved at the top of them. These were the graves of the middling to well-to-do folks. Poorer people had simple pottery shells. The poorest, of course, had nothing.

Apart from the dust devils and heat spirals flitting over the tombs, there was little to see. Owen scrutinized the area carefully to satisfy the sheikh and Ali Marwash but didn't really expect to see anything significant. The main purpose of being up there was to keep an eye on the constables, who might otherwise have joined the general search for shade.

They were not having much luck with their search. Owen had expected to find the girl's body relatively quickly. Surely the arms runners wouldn't have gone to the trouble of taking the body away with them?

But as time went by and no body was found, that increasingly appeared to be what they had done.

The constables, even with Owen's eye on them, were definitely lagging. He saw a suspicious human gap, got down from his vantage point and went over. The constable was, as he had expected, sitting down.

"By God, it is hot!" said the offender, looking up at him.

"By God, it will be hotter for you if you do not soon get on your feet!" said Owen.

The man grinned and rejoined the searching. Owen had some sympathy. He had seen the sweat running down the man's face, could feel it running down his own.

Back near the tomb Georgiades was also sitting down. He had taken out a handkerchief and was mopping his neck.

"Why go to hell when you can have it here?" he said to Owen, before rising to his feet and shambling off.

Georgiades was on a patrol of his own, sniffing round the tombs. Owen let him carry on. The Greek usually knew what he was doing.

Owen, too, felt like sitting down. The sheikh and Ali Marwash *had* sat down. He went over to talk to them, using it as a pretext to squat for a moment himself.

"Alas!" he said to Ali Marwash. "It begins to look as if those evil men have taken your daughter's body further afield than I had thought."

"Why should they go to the trouble?" asked the sheikh.

Why indeed? thought Owen. A body was surely as conspicuous as a load of arms.

Georgiades came and hovered. When Owen stood up, he turned and walked quietly away. Owen walked back casually in the general direction of the girl's tomb. Georgiades suddenly appeared beside him.

"Want to come and look?" he asked.

He led Owen to a tomb some distance away from where they had found the arms cache. It was a big square family tomb and had obviously been built some years ago, for the sand had drifted halfway up the sides. The headstones on top drooped towards each other.

"Old grave, new work," said Georgiades.

He took Owen round to the entrance. It looked intact. The roofing stones were still in position over the entrance house and sand was piled over the top.

But there was something odd about it. It didn't quite fit the pattern of drift. And there, to one side, were distinct spade marks, still not yet filled by the drifting sand.

Owen stood looking at it.

"Do you want me to open it?" asked Georgiades.

Some way across the cemetery a little party of men, supposed to be searching, came to a stop and stood for a moment talking. One or two of them looked idly in Owen's direction. Beyond them he could see another party. And, just coming into sight were some constables scanning the ground half-heartedly.

"No," he said.

They came back just before it grew dark. The vast cemetery was deserted. Only in the far distance was there any movement, a woman walking home between the tombs, a great water pot on her head.

In the pockets of air between the tombs it was still hot, but the glare had gone out of the sun and the soft evening light was easy on the eyes.

They had come properly equipped with spades and the wooden half-baskets used in Egypt for scooping and carrying soil. It would not take them long. And this time there would be no crowds of onlookers to interfere.

He ordered the men to start work.

They quickly scraped the sand from the roofstones and lifted them off. One of the smaller men climbed into the entrance house and wrestled away the large stone which blocked the entrance to the main chamber. Somebody handed him down a lamp. He held it out into the tomb and peered inside.

But already Owen knew. As the stone was pulled away from the entrance the smell of new corruption reached up to him.

The man with the lamp pulled the folds of his galabeah over his nose and mouth. Then he looked again.

He gave a startled exclamation and jumped back. In a second he came scrambling up out of the entrance house.

"Effendi!" he said, his eyes wide open with shock. "Effendi!"

"What is it?"

The man could hardly speak for a moment.

"Effendi!" he said at last. "Effendi! Not one but—two!"

⁄₥₥⁊

Owen went down himself, holding a handkerchief over his face. It took a little while for his eyes to get used to the flickering shadows cast by the lamp. Besides, his vision was impeded by something.

Eventually he made out what it was. A girl's body, not lying on its right side and supported on bricks as was proper, but cast higgledy-piggledy across the floor of the tomb.

And then, further away, he saw the other thing that had shocked the man. It was another body, clearly recent, also thrown in anyhow, and also of a girl.

This body had not even been prepared for interment. It was still in its ordinary workaday clothes. The clothes were deeply stained with ugly dark patches but had not yet had time to rot away and he could see what they were.

In the half light it was hard to tell, but—

"Shintiyan," he said. "She's wearing shintiyan."

"Color?" asked Georgiades.

⁄₥₥⁊

"But, laddie, I'm busy!" protested the pathologist.

Owen had caught the eminent man just as he was going to lunch. Lunch was important to Cairns-Grant and he approached it with the single-minded devotion which had made the Cairo forensic laboratory, despite its lack of size and facilities, one of the leaders in its field. It was also, of course, that it had plenty of practice.

"Better even than Chicago," Cairns-Grant was wont to say fondly. Cairo, he was prone to point out to visiting Americans, was the murder capital of the world, with a higher rate of homicide than any other major city. And he regarded Owen with considerable affections for what he considered his contribution to this desirable state of affairs.

"A brief word!" pleaded Owen.

Cairns-Grant looked at his watch.

"I was going to the Club," he said. "Would you care to join me?"

Owen sometimes went to the Sporting Club himself for lunch, but that was only if he was in that part of the city. Cairns-Grant went every day. It was about half an hour's drive in an arabeah from the Government Laboratories but Cairns-Grant justified it on the grounds that in the middle of the day, considering the nature of the work, it was too hot to continue working. "They thaw," he explained, "so quickly," and no one felt drawn to explore the matter further.

Cairns-Grant's lunchtime conversations tended to be full of this kind of grisly detail and today was no exception.

"Ye see," he said, "when a body is left long in water, or buried in damp ground, it changes. Human fat, which is normally semifluid, is converted into firm fat. Like mutton suet," he explained kindly.

Mutton was on the menu.

"No, thanks," Owen said to the waiter. "I'll have fish."

"Oh, there you are," said a voice. "I was hoping to catch you."

Owen looked up. It was Garvin, an old card-playing crony of Cairns-Grant's.

"Mind if I join you?"

"Do." The waiter rushed to lay another place. "I was just explaining to young Owen here about adipocere."

"Adipocere?"

"Human fat," said Cairns-Grant, "in dead bodies."

"Oh," said Garvin, studying the menu.

"It's to do with the body he's just brought in. He's a guid lad," said Cairns-Grant fondly. "He brings me in a lot of cases."

"Mutton, I think," said Garvin, closing the menu with a snap. "What's this one?"

"A lady who's been in the river. Not for very long, I'd say, judging by the limited adipocere. But definitely long enough to start the process. Of course, it depends on temperature to some extent. Now up here in Cairo—"

Cairns-Grant went happily on.

"What did she die of?" asked Garvin when Cairns-Grant paused for a moment to draw breath.

"I was just telling you. You see, the hyoid—that's the small bone at the base of the tongue—was fractured in two places, one at the top of the left horn, the other where the right horn joined the body. The point is," said Cairns-Grant, "that there was some adipocere—limited, mind—in the fractured ends of the hyoid."

"Which means?" said Garvin.

Cairns-Grant was slightly taken aback.

"It's obvious, isn't it? The fracturing took place before immersion in the water. Haven't I made myself clear?" he said worriedly.

"Yes, yes, yes, yes," Owen hastily reassured him. "Only—"

"You see," Cairns-Grant explained to Garvin, "there's often some degree of fracturing in the bodies we get. Especially those"—he gave Owen a proud glance—"we get from young Owen."

"So what you're saying," said Owen, "is that the fracturing took place while she was still on board?"

"On board?" said Garvin.

"Aye," said Cairns-Grant.

"Any idea what caused it?"

"Didn't ye look?" said Cairns-Grant, surprised.

"Not closely."

"Closely enough, I daresay," said Cairns-Grant. "Well, ye're right to be cautious ahead of the pathologist's report. If only more of your ilk would do the same. Rushing to conclusions ahead of the evidence! That's often the problem."

"So what did she die of?" asked Garvin.

"Oh, she was garotted. The cord was still around the neck."

"Garotted!" said Owen.

"Oh, garotted," said Garvin indifferently. "We get plenty of those. How do you come to be involved?" he asked Owen.

Garotting might be a staple of ordinary police work but it was not something that Owen, as Political Officer, was normally concerned with.

"It's that Sekhmet case. You remember, the girl on the dahabeeyah—Narouz's dahabeeyah."

Garvin put down his knife and fork.

"Garotte!" he said. "I don't like the sound of that! We wouldn't want *that* to come out!"

⦿〰〰⦿

"Garotte!" said Paul, perturbed. "This is really very awkward. We're just coming up to the final session, with any luck. The Agreement's due to be signed next week. After that we'll be home and dry."

⦿〰〰⦿

"Garotte!" whispered Zeinab. "That is horrible!"

She had a little weep. Owen put his arm around her. She let it rest there.

Suddenly she threw it off.

"What are you going to do about it?" she demanded.

"Well, I'm—"

"That's not enough! Get it out of them!"

"Get what out of who?"

"The truth. Someone must know. The Rais, the eunuch, Narouz—"

"I'm trying to get it out of them."

"You're not. You're too soft, too nice, too gentle. Oh, I love you"—Owen thought this at least was improvement—"but you are too weak." He changed his mind. "This is Egypt."

"What exactly did you have in mind? Amputation?"

"That will do for a start," said Zeinab.

"Right!" Owen sprang to his feet. "Limbs, testicles and entrails! On the table tomorrow morning!"

He made to start for the door.

Zeinab looked at him uncertainly.

⚭

"Garotte!" said Prince Narouz, looking shaken. "Are you sure?"

"Yes."

"That's awful!" The Prince shook his head. "Awful!"

"Yes."

"You're absolutely certain?" he asked again. "I mean, there's no possibility—"

"The cord was round her neck."

The Prince winced.

"That's awful!" he said again. "Awful!"

"We can be certain about these things," said Owen, "now that we have the body."

"Yes, yes, of course." The Prince put his hand to his head. "It's just that...Death, I was prepared for, we know about that. But garotte!" He shuddered. "It's awful, horrible!"

A thought suddenly struck him.

"But isn't that an unusual way of killing someone?"

"Very common in Cairo."

"No, no. I don't mean that. I mean, if people quarrel, or have a fight, that's not what they do to each other. They hit each other, or stab each other, or..."

His voice trailed away.

"It's a professional way of killing, if that's what you mean. There are people who specialize in it."

"But—but—how could a person like that be on board the dahabeeyah?"

"You tell me," said Owen, and waited.

The Prince moistened his lips.

"I—I don't know."

"The dahabeeyah is a small place, you see. A stranger—a stranger like that—would be bound to be noticed. He would be conspicious, wouldn't he?"

"There are places to hide," muttered the Prince, "even on the dahabeeyah."

"And then, why was he on board in the first place? Perhaps you could tell me that, Prince Narouz?"

The Prince put his hand to his head again.

"I can't think," he whispered. "I can't think. There's no reason—there could be no reason."

"Do you think he would go to that trouble, that risk, for no reason?"

"I don't know," said Narouz wretchedly.

"He would have to be well-paid, wouldn't he? And hired beforehand. Which makes it, well, premeditated, doesn't it?"

Narouz appeared in a state of shock.

"It couldn't be," he said, "it just couldn't be."

"These are questions," said Owen, "to which I would like answers. And I was hoping you would be able to help me."

Narouz put both hands to his head.

"I would if I could," he said desperately. "But I can't! It's—it couldn't have happened that way! I must think! I must think!"

"Yes," said Owen, "you must."

ᘓ᙮᙭ᙰᘏ

"Well," said Mahmoud, pouring Owen some more coffee, "you're quite right. You don't have to be a professional to garotte people but the chances are you are!"

"This one was. Cairns-Grant says there's a difference in the way you garotte people between a professional and an amateur.

The amateur just wraps a cord round the throat and pulls as hard as he can. The professional knows just where to apply the pressure. It's a much quicker job. The marking is quite different."

"Well, if it was professional, that alters things quite a bit."

"Yes, it rules out a quarrel and then a blow or perhaps even a push."

"Yes, it means it had to be thought about beforehand and a killer hired and brought on board."

"That puzzles me a bit. If it's Narouz. Why would he want to go to the length of bringing someone on board especially to do the killing when he must have known this would immediately direct attention on him and he could so easily have arranged for it to happen somewhere else?"

"There's the question of motive, too," said Mahmoud, waving away a fly. "The most likely explanation of the girl's death was always a quarrel on board, followed, as you said, by a blow or a push. But that's ruled out if it's premeditated, and it must be something else."

"And if it's something else, why do it on board?"

They were in one of the shopping centers of the city and the street was filling up after the afternoon siesta. The lengthening shadows were bringing people out of their houses for that universal Mediterranean evening promenade.

Even Mahmoud, very un-Cairene in that he seemed to blaze with energy all day, was Cairene enough to expand and relax almost visibly as the evening came on.

"How's Zeinab?" he asked mellowly.

"The same. She's not moved an inch. She can be very inflexible sometimes."

"Ah well," murmured Mahmoud commiseratingly.

"Of course, she was very upset when I told her it was garotte."

"Unpleasant," said Mahmoud. "Nasty."

"No, no, it wasn't so much that. She fired up. She said I was too soft."

"What did she expect you to do?"

"Castrate them, I think."

"Anyone particular?"

"Narouz, his Rais, the crew in general—"

"Well, she has a point, hasn't she?"

"I don't think I'd go as far as that," said Owen dubiously.

"They must have known," said Mahmoud. "You couldn't have somebody like that on board without them knowing. There are no hiding places on a dahabeeyah so far as the crew are concerned. It's a small space. It wouldn't be possible to keep out of their way. Someone must have seen him."

"They won't say anything. They're loyal to Narouz."

"Of course," said Mahmoud, "we could always try someone who's not loyal to Narouz!"

⌘

"It's been a long time," said the Belgian girl, Nanette.

"I've had other sweethearts to attend to," said Owen.

"What about him?" asked Nanette, pointing to Mahmoud. "Has he got other sweethearts, too?"

Mahmoud, straitlaced and not at all sure about all this, looked uncomfortable.

The girls laughed.

They were meeting in the girls' *appartement*.

"We don't usually do business here," said Masha, the Hungarian one. "We're making an exception for you."

"Thank you," said Owen. He had passed them a note at the gambling salon where they worked, thinking that this time he would not approach them through the manager in case it caused them problems.

The girls were used to receiving notes. On his way out a reply was tucked in his pocket. It was on scented paper and in a little mauve envelope and invited him round to the girls' flat the following day.

The flat was soft and cushioned and had two low divans. Nanette sat on one and invited Mahmoud to sit beside her. Masha lay on the other and made a little space for Owen.

"How much are you prepared to pay?" asked Nanette.

"Pay?" said Mahmoud.

Owen shook his head.

"I'm afraid that's not what I had in mind," he said apologetically. "We're here on business. Remember? That incident on the river."

"That? We'd thought you'd solved that long ago!"

"Still a few questions."

"Oh dear!" Nanette pulled a long face. "We've told you all we know. Can't we talk about something else?"

"You still ought to pay," said Masha. "Our knowledge is priceless."

"There is no question of payment," said Mahmoud severely. "It is a question of duty under the law."

Masha made a *moue.*

"You behave yourself!" said Mahmoud. "This is the Mamur Zapt. He can deport you from the country."

"Oh dear," said Masha. "From Egypt? That would really hurt. Can I say where I want to go, please?" she asked Owen.

"Let's get back to the point," said Owen.

"Right!"

Both girls sprang up and sat to attention on the divans.

Mahmoud seemed about to explode.

"Relax, sweetie," said Nanette, patting him on the hand. "It's only a joke!"

"Can I ask you some questions?" said Owen hastily.

"It is about this girl, yes?" asked Masha.

"Yes. Can we go back to the night you were picked up at Beni Suef. Was anyone else picked up with you?"

"The girl."

"Apart from her?"

The girls looked at each other.

"I don't think so."

"There was just the boatman."

"Was he one of the crew?"

"Yes. Abdul."

"He took you out to the dahabeeyah."

"Yes. It was a little rowing boat."

"Was there anyone else waiting at the landing stage? Someone he might have gone back for?"

The girls looked at each other again.

"It was dark. We didn't really see anyone."

"OK. Now can you think hard and see if you can remember anyone else coming on board? Not at Beni Suef but anywhere else?"

"What sort of person?"

"An Arab. Not a member of the crew."

"Lots. When we were at Luxor, lots came on board. They were carrying things. Food, water, that sort of thing."

"Did any of them stay on board?"

The girls looked doubtful.

"Honestly, how would we know?"

"Did you see anyone strange? You must have got to know the crew."

"We knew everybody, more or less. By the end, at any rate."

"And there was no one who suddenly appeared and you saw for the first time?"

"I don't remember anyone like that," said Masha. "Why do you ask?"

Owen thought, then decided to tell them.

"Because Leila was garotted."

"Garotted!"

"That's not very nice, is it? You mean, while we were on board—?"

"Yes."

"Jesus!"

"It could have been us," said Masha.

"I feel like a drink," said Nanette. She went out of the room and came back with a bottle of whisky and some glasses.

"No, thank you," said Mahmoud.

"Some coffee? I'll make you some. I could do with some myself."

Mahmoud accepted a cup politely, then felt obliged to over-respond and praised its flavor, sweetness, etcetera, copiously.

The girls understood.

"Don't mind us," said Nanette, putting her hand on his knee. "Sorry about the drink. But I do need it!"

She poured herself a stiff glass.

"Garotte!" she said. "Holy Mary!"

Masha helped herself to some of the coffee.

"We didn't see anyone like that," she said. "If that's what you've been asking us."

"You couldn't tell," said Nanette. "They look the same as anyone else."

"A strange face," said Owen. "He'd be a little apart from the crew."

They shook their heads.

"We didn't see anyone like that. Honest!"

"Just imagine!" said Nanette.

"A good job we stuck together," said Masha.

"She was on her own, of course."

"Well, that's what she wanted. She could have stayed with us."

"To be fair, we weren't too welcoming."

"She preferred it that way. Even when she had the chance, she would go off on her own."

"That was it, wasn't it? She was up there on her own."

"You think that was it?"

"Yes. If it had been one of us, it would have been the same."

"Jesus!" Masha shuddered. "It could have been me!"

"I think he was looking for Leila," said Owen.

"What, especially?"

Owen nodded.

Nanette took another drink.

"Well, I don't know what makes you say that," she said, "but I'd prefer it to be that way. No hard feelings about Leila, that's terrible! But all the same I'm glad he was looking for one particular woman and not any."

Masha poured some of the whisky into Owen's coffee and took a sip.

"I don't know which is worse," she said. "Someone who is crazy or someone who isn't."

"They'd have to have a motive," said Nanette.

"We were hoping you might be able to help us on that," said Owen.

"There weren't any quarrels, if that's what you mean."

"In fact, rather the reverse. He put himself out for her, didn't he?"

"Who?"

"The Prince, Narouz. He was rather nice to her, I thought. Kept trying to get her to join in."

"Of course, there was Fahid."

"He doesn't really count, though."

"He was pestering her."

"Yes, but I mean—!" Both girls laughed.

"Still, he kept on to her. That's why she went up there on her own."

"Yes, but she could have pushed him off, couldn't she?"

"I thought at one time he might have pushed *her* off. I thought that might be it. Not meaning, to, really, just being overkeen."

"Well, it wouldn't have been that, would it? I mean, garotte!"

"Fahid was keen on her, was he?" asked Owen.

"When he found out," said Nanette.

"Found out?"

"Found out what women were for."

"I don't understand," said Owen.

Masha caressed his neck.

"I'll give you some lessons," she offered.

"I know that bit. But what's that got to do with Fahid?"

The two girls looked at him in astonishment.

"Don't you know? That was the whole point of the boat trip."

Chapter 10

"I suppose," said Narouz, "I have to confess."

They were sitting again on the terrace of the Continental. Owen had suggested he visit the Prince at home but Narouz had rejected that in favor of the hotel. He preferred to make his confessions in the open air.

"Yes," he said, rolling the ice in his glass and looking down, a trifle wistfully, at the Street of the Camel, "I should have told you before. Only there are some things"—he shifted his gaze to Owen—"that it's difficult to talk about."

"It would surely have been better—" began Owen.

The Prince held up his hand.

"You're absolutely right, my dear fellow. Only one doesn't always see these things at the time. It seemed a simple family matter. Dynastic, one might say. And, therefore, if you'll forgive me"—he patted Owen on the arm—"nothing to do with the Mamur Zapt."

"Something to do with a clearly criminal matter."

"But was it, my dear fellow? Really? Incidental, I would have said. Only incidental."

"That remains to be seen."

The Prince regarded him closely.

"You're surely not still thinking—?"

"At the moment," said Owen, "I see no reason for dismissing the possibility."

"But garotte, my dear fellow! Garotte!"

The Prince started to extend an arm, as if to invite Owen to share the impossibility of it, but thought better and withdrew it.

"It's out of the question," he said quietly.

"It exists as a possibility," said Owen, "until I've heard enough to be able to discard it."

"He's just a boy," said the Prince.

"Carry on," said Owen.

The Prince shrugged.

"Well, that was it. Still a boy. At his age! I don't know what they were doing. They keep them in the harem so long these days! In my time—" The Prince sighed.

"You're not telling me they've kept him in the harem till now!"

"As good as. Oh, he has his own quarters, his own servants. But they're all picked by his mother and report daily to her. Can you imagine that? Daily! A report on all his doings. Bowel movements included, it wouldn't surprise me."

The Prince looked gloomily at Owen.

"Well, of course, things couldn't go on like that. The boy is, after all, an heir to the throne. A distant one, it is true—he comes after me—but nevertheless an heir. It was time he grew up."

He dropped his voice conspiratorially.

"I don't mind telling you, old chap—but it's between ourselves—there were the most frightful arguments between his mother and the Khedive. Between ourselves, I think the old boy's a bit afraid of her. Of course, he had to insist—I mean, it was his duty, wasn't it? He has, after all, a responsibility to the throne."

Owen was slightly losing the thread.

"What exactly did he insist *on?*" he asked.

"Well, first it was that Fahid had to be—simply *had* to be—prepared for his royal duties. The boy was an absolute ignoramus. You won't believe this, my dear fellow," said the

Prince earnestly, touching Owen confidentially on the arm, "but he actually didn't know where Alexandria was, never mind Cannes!"

Owen tut-tutted.

"Yes," said the Prince, gratified, "and as for all that economics stuff! Not an idea! Of course, I would not say that I myself had a total grasp of the subject but it is important, especially for a Khedive, to know enough to at least be able to borrow intelligently. But that, of course, was not the worst of it."

"No?" said Owen, seeing that he was expected to.

"No." The Prince dropped his voice even lower. "*He had never known a woman.*"

The Prince looked at Owen, confident of his response.

"What?" said Owen, more bewildered than shocked.

The Prince took it for shock.

"Well, yes," he said. "That's how I felt, too. You'd think, with all those women in the harem—! But, of course, they were all under his mother's eye. Even so, you would have thought—!"

The Prince shook his head despairingly.

"What is human nature coming to these degenerate days! Why, in my day, there were women eager enough. After all, surely it is something to be proud of, initiating an heir to the throne into the ways of manhood? Even at the age of eight."

"Eight?"

The Prince shrugged his shoulders modestly.

"I suppose I was advanced for my years. But that only made it more pleasurable for everybody. Of course, when my mother found out, she had me out of the harem in a hurry."

"The Khedive—"

"Pleased, my dear fellow. Pleased, rather than the reverse. Regarded it as a sign of maturity."

"And Prince Fahid?"

"Not like that at all." The Prince looked despairing again. "I really fear there's something wrong with the boy. When I

20

found out, I went to the Khedive at once. I said, look, something must be done about this. Well, naturally he agreed with me. So—" He paused to draw breath.

"So?"

He looked at Owen gravely. "The Khedive asked me to take the duty upon myself."

"The duty—?"

"Of seeing that he was initiated into manhood."

"And this was the real purpose of the trip to Luxor?"

"Exactly. He would be under my eye all the time, he would be away from his mother, I could supply the necessary women, a range of them, to make the whole thing easier—but there again, my dear fellow, what difficulty! I had really not anticipated—! The lack of taste, my dear fellow!"

"Nanette and Masha?"

"The old Continental tradition: an older woman inducting the young man. It's better like that. They're more patient. I thought, too, that he ought to start with someone relatively sophisticated. It sets standards right from the start!"

"Leila?"

The Prince hesitated.

"Well, that, I admit, was partly for my own gratification. A little extra piquancy, you know, the most modest Egyptian woman just coming out of her shell. A different flavor, unusual. But wasted, my dear fellow, wasted on him!"

"I thought," said Owen, making the connection with what the girls had said, "that she was the one he went for? That his preference for her was rather marked?"

"Yes," said the Prince gloomily, "but for the wrong reasons. He ran to her in flight, my dear fellow, flight from experience—not pursuit of it."

"Nanette and Masha frightened him?"

"Yes," said the Prince dejectedly. "There you have it. He ran to Leila as to a mother." The Prince shuddered. "It's his mother again. That damned woman! She's a lot to answer for."

Owen thought it over. It didn't quite square.

"I thought it wasn't quite like that," he said. "I thought he actively pursued her."

"Like a child his mother," said the Prince sadly.

"I don't think so. Not from what I heard."

The Prince looked up in hope.

"You mean—?"

"So I heard."

"Genuine sexual passion?"

"That's the impression I got."

"Well," said the Prince, cheering up. "That certainly makes it a lot better."

"Hardly," Owen pointed out. "The girl died."

"Yes, but—you're not suggesting, my dear fellow, she died resisting his advances?"

"I was wondering."

The Prince, now cheered up enormously, summoned another drink.

"To be truthful, old chap," he said confidingly, "I did wonder that myself. But I saw it slightly differently. I thought he might have tried to put his arms round her—I saw it as a forlorn hope—and through sheer clumsiness—the boy is *extremely* maladroit—knocked her overboard. Caught her off balance, perhaps. It's easily done, especially on a boat."

"I don't think so," said Owen. "She was garotted."

"I didn't know that at the time. I feared the worst."

"Worst?"

"That the foolish boy might have killed her somehow. Probably by accident."

"You don't think that now?"

"Of course not. Garotting requires manual skill, my dear fellow, something that Fahid patently has not got. He would probably have garotted himself if he had tried."

"I am afraid it still has to remain a possibility," Owen insisted.

The Prince dismissed it with a wave of his hand.

"I think you can safely forget about that, old chap," he said confidently. "In fact, you can forget about the whole thing now."

"I don't think so. The girl died."

"At least Fahid was nothing to do with it," said Narouz.

ᏰᎷᎽᏰ

His mind now more at ease on both counts, Fahid's sexuality and also his possible culpability over Leila, Narouz agreed readily enough to Owen talking to his nephew.

"You may get more out of him than I," he said. "These days he seems increasingly afflicted with dumbness whenever I am present."

He arranged, again, for them to meet at the Continental.

"It will be good experience for him," he said, "mixing with ordinary people."

The Continental suited Owen, who was meeting Zeinab there himself. Zeinab had not yet appeared and he was sitting alone at a table on the terrace when Narouz arrived with his charge.

"Do see what you can get out of him," he whispered as he left. "Was it real sexual passion or not?"

That was roughly the sort of question Owen had in mind, so he said he would. When he found himself faced by the shy, gazellelike boy, however, the issue was unexpectedly difficult to broach.

He asked Fahid about the two girls, Masha and Nanette: had Fahid liked them?

The Prince shrugged in a way like his uncle. Liking clearly did not come into it. Owen got the impression, as he probed, that the boy stood rather in awe of them.

As, indeed, he did with regard to most adults. He listened to Owen respectfully but rather like a small boy listening to a headmaster. The possibility of a man-to-man conversation on the lines Narouz expected seemed remote.

Owen asked about Leila. Fahid was noncommittal. So noncommittal that it was plain he wasn't putting into words anything he felt at all. He replied to Owen's questions politely and dutifully but evaded firmly any attempt by Owen to establish a kind of intimacy.

Owen felt increasing desperation and it was with some relief that he saw Zeinab approaching them along the terrace.

The Prince rose politely. Harem-schooled he might be, but somewhere along the line someone had introduced him to Western styles of social intercourse.

Zeinab, moving easily into the French idiom current among the Cairene upper classes, shook hands.

"We have met," she said, "but it was a long time ago and I don't expect you remember me."

Owen was grateful that she had not mentioned the harem, which was where she had probably met him. Zeinab, as the daughter of a senior Pasha, was on visiting terms with the Khedive's family, or, at least, its female members. Now that she had arrived, however, the prospect of a man-to-man exchange of confidence seemed to have vanished altogether.

The Prince murmured something noncommittal. He looked at Zeinab, however, with curiosity. She was clearly Egyptian and clearly a lady of rank but she did not quite fit into any of the categories he was familiar with.

Zeinab remarked that she had been talking to his mother the week before. The Prince asked cautiously about her health.

Owen watched the boy working out how to handle Zeinab. The French style gave him the clue. He would treat her as a foreigner. He responded to her conversational initiatives in much the way he had to Owen's.

Zeinab soon registered this. She had been asking him about the trip on the dahabeeyah but now she fell silent. Owen saw her thinking.

Suddenly she pounced.

"Was Leila the sort of girl your mother would have approved of?"

"No," said the Prince immediately, caught off guard. "No," he added on consideration, a trifle grimly.

"She didn't approve of the whole thing, did she?"

"No."

"What about you? I expect you quite liked the idea, didn't you?"

"At first."

"But then not. Was it those women?"

The Prince tried to find a bland reply but could not. He muttered something.

Zeinab leaned forward and put her hand gently on his arm. The Prince flinched slightly. It was normal in Arab conversation for men to touch—in fact, if they didn't, it struck people as cold—but for a woman to do so, unless she was family, was immodest.

Zeinab kept her hand there, however, and switched from French to the more intimate Arabic.

"I expect they did not know how to behave," she said.

"No," the Prince admitted.

"But Leila knew how to behave, I expect."

"Yes," said the Prince unwillingly.

"Because she was Egyptian and they were foreign."

"That's right," the boy muttered.

Still keeping her hand on his arm, Zeinab shifted her chair closer to him. Then she slipped her hand quite naturally round him so that it was almost as if she was giving him a sisterly hug.

Or a maternal hug, Owen suddenly realized.

"Leila knew how to behave," said Zeinab softly. "She wasn't like them."

"No," said the boy.

"She oughtn't to have been on that boat. It wasn't the place for her."

"No."

"Why was she on it?"

"It was him," said the boy. "He made her."

"Ah, that's what it was! Did she talk to you about it?"

"No, I wanted her to but she wouldn't. I asked her to but she—she said I was too young and didn't understand these things."

"She wanted to spare you, I expect. I'm sure she knew how you felt about her."

Fahid was silent.

"Did you tell her how you felt?"

"Yes," said Fahid. His face began to work. All the calm indifference was gone.

"She spurned me," he said. "She told me to go away."

"That was not spurning you. She wanted to spare you."

"No, no, it was spurning. She—she laughed at me!"

"Surely not!"

"Yes. Yes. And then I hated her. I ran away and cursed her. I didn't want anything to do with her. She despised me and she loved him!"

"I don't think she despised you," said Zeinab gently.

"She preferred him."

"These things happen. But I'm sure she didn't want to be unkind to you."

"She had given herself to him."

"But not to you?"

"No," said the boy, "although—although I wanted her to."

"The others did?"

"Ah yes," said the boy, with a dismissive gesture, "but that was not the same."

"No, of course not. It's not the same when you're not in love."

"But she did it," said the boy fiercely. "She did it with him."

"She was in love."

"No, she wasn't!"

"She preferred him," said Zeinab gently. "You told me so yourself."

"Ah, but that doesn't mean she was in love with him. She only preferred him because she thought he might be Khedive."

"Well," said Zeinab, "perhaps so."

"She didn't love him," the boy insisted. "She was very unhappy. Afterwards, she went away by herself. He tried to get her to come down but she wouldn't!"

"This was that last day," asked Owen, "when she was alone on the top deck?"

"Yes. It was dinnertime and she wouldn't come down. Narouz went up, I went up—"

"You went up?"

"Yes. I thought she might listen to me."

"I thought you hated her?"

"I did, but—but—I wanted to see her."

"What did you say to her?"

"I said: 'Come down, Leila, it's dinnertime.' But she said she wouldn't, she would never come down. It was him, you see," the boy said passionately. "She didn't want to see him. She felt ashamed. She said she had cheapened herself. She said men were all like that. There was another man she thought had loved her but when it came down to it, all he'd wanted was the same thing. He hadn't objected when Narouz had asked her to come on the dahabeeyah, he had encouraged her, he had said that sort of thing didn't matter. But she had said it did matter. But she had gone all the same because he had said it would be better if she did go. But now she was sorry because she knew it wasn't a good idea, but it was too late."

The boy's shoulders were shaking. Zeinab tightened her arm round him.

"She *did* talk to you, then, didn't she?" she said softly.

"No," said the boy. "She told me to go away, that I was like the rest of them, she pushed me away—"

"Pushed?"

"I tried to take her hand."

"Was that all?"

"I put my arm round her," said the boy defiantly. The defiance lasted only a moment. His face puckered. "But she pushed me away!"

"What did you do then?" asked Owen very quietly.

"Do?" The boy's face blinked up at him in surprise. "Do? I came down, of course."

ᏼᎶ

Mahmoud had rung Owen suggesting they meet for coffee. He had spent the whole day interviewing the crew of the dahabeeyah once again and was understandably exhausted.

"Get anywhere?" asked Owen.

Mahmoud had been checking whether any of them had seen an unauthorized person on board. All swore blind that they had seen no one.

"Of course they could just be covering up," he said, "but I don't think so."

They were sitting in a café at the end of the Mussky, just where the street comes out into the Ataba el Khadra.

The Ataba was the starting place for most of Cairo's trams and was in many respects the epitome of all that was modern and ungracious in the city. Somnolent two-horse arabeahs gave way to strident, bell-ringing trams. Sleepy, open-fronted shops yielded place to brazen emporia selling the latest line in European hosiery. And here, instead of doing nothing, which was the usual Cairene pursuit, everyone was hurrying to catch a tram or else touting for business.

The two chief trades in the Ataba were the selling of pastries and the dissemination of seditious literature.

As one such disseminator passed him, Owen automatically stuck out his hand. The seller removed the piastres from his palm and replaced them by a whole wad of newspapers and pamphlets.

He glanced at the top page. Leering up at him was a scurrilous cartoon of Prince Narouz.

He put the wad on the table and picked up the paper with the cartoon and examined it more closely.

The whole of the front page was devoted to an attack on the Prince as a modernizer, a lackey of Great Britain and general betrayer of the Egyptian cause. Even now, it was said, he was working to sign away Egyptian rights under a new secret Agreement which the Khedive was about to conclude with the British.

The writer was indeed well informed. In reviewing the Prince's personal morals, or lack of, reference was made to a recent trip by dahabeeyah undertaken for lewd lascivious purposes. The voyage, it added, had ended tragically with the death in suspicious circumstances of a well-connected but foolish Egyptian girl lured on to the boat under false pretenses.

The article did not say directly that Narouz had a hand in the girl's death; it did not need to.

Owen passed the paper over to Mahmoud. Mahmoud read the article and shrugged.

"It's come out, then," he said.

Owen turned the paper over and looked for its imprint. It had none. "It's illicit, of course."

He could censor only material which was legally published. Illegal publications, with which Cairo abounded, had to be hit at by raiding the printer. It was, however, usually hit and miss.

"Do you recognize the press?"

"I don't; Nikos probably will."

He folded the paper and put it in his pocket.

"If they didn't see anyone," he said, reverting to the crew of the dahabeeyah, "that probably means there was no one there. You couldn't hide on board for long. Not without someone seeing you."

"The last stop was Luxor. They would have had to have hidden up for nearly a week."

"It's possible. But unlikely."

"I agree. But, you see, that raises an interesting question. What if the garotter was not on board at all? What if he knew where the dahabeeyah was going to tie up? What if he was on shore, waiting?"

༄

Owen attended in person the reinterment of Ali Marwash's daughter. This was considered a great honor, indeed, almost disproportionately so, since the deceased was only a woman.

There had already been difficulties over the ceremony which should accompany the reburial. Ali Marwash had wanted another full-scale funeral service but this had been vetoed on the grounds that it would have to take place in the mosque and the body was hardly in a condition for that.

Besides, there were theological issues. At what point had the body been moved from the tomb? Before the examining angels, Munkar and Nekeer, had concluded their examination or after? In the latter case the soul might have already departed, either to the place where good souls await the Last Day or to the prison where evil souls are confined to await their doom. In each case the prayers would need to be different.

The issue was carefully weighed and, as is often the case with such issues, not easily resolved. Meanwhile, the girl remained parted from her tomb. Might not the visiting angels grow impatient?

Agreement was eventually reached on a brief ceremony at the grave followed by a Sebhah at the father's house. Here there was another difficulty, for Ali Marwash wanted a full-scale Sebhah whereas the local Imam thought that was unnecessary, the deceased having already had the benefit of a substantial Sebhah and, anyway, being only a woman. They compromised on a reduced Sebhah, which, in Owen's view, was just as well, for a full Sebhah lasted four hours. He had intended going only to the ceremony at the grave but when the palm branch had been broken over the tomb and the fiki had recited the last prayer Ali Marwash had approached him and invited him to be present at the Sebhah.

Owen felt strongly as a matter of principle that it was important for people like him to join in the activities of the community when asked; otherwise the British would never gain acceptance. Besides, he felt great sympathy with the girl's shattered parents. He thanked Ali Marwash and said he would be glad to accept.

Back at the house he squatted cross-legged on a cushion and was fed pastries and sweet cakes while the fiki settled to his work. There was only one fiki; that had been part of the compromise. In a rich man's house there might be as many as ten. It was the fiki who had participated in the ceremonies on the previous occasion.

He registered Owen's presence and turned away slightly. Owen shrugged. He didn't have to be liked by everybody. He remembered seeing the fiki in the courtyard. On that occasion, as on this, he had seemed to be organizing the proceedings. He was obviously a prominent figure in the neighborhood, although the post of fiki was not in itself especially important.

The fiki recited several chapters from the Koran and then passed on to the prayers, first taking up the sebhah itself, which was a necklace of a thousand beads. Some of the prayers had to be repeated—as many as a hundred times—and the beads were used for counting the repetitions.

Owen knew his Koran but not, of course, as well as the other guests, many of whom knew at least the opening Suras by heart, having learned them as children in the local kuttub, or school.

There were several children in the room and as the evening wore on, and the supply of cakes increased, they became more and more in evidence. When the fiki had finished his recitations and the occasion had turned into a general wake or party, the little boys flitted among the guests, offered sweetmeats by all and sundry.

Owen overheard Georgiades talking to one of the boys.

"You look a big chap," said Georgiades. "Do you go to the kuttub yet?"

"Oh yes," said the boy, "I've been going for a long time now."

"Does the master beat you?"

"Sometimes." The boy pointed to the fiki. "He's my master."

"Really?"

"Well, there's another master most of the time, but he's the one I like."

"He comes to teach you your Suras, does he?"

"That's right. I like him because sometimes he gets us invited to sing at funerals and then we get lots of sweets and cakes."

"Did you sing at this funeral?"

"Yes."

"The first time? When the body was carried to the tomb?"

"Yes. But I might have done anyway because my uncle is Ali Marwash's cousin."

"There were several of you from the kuttub, were there?"

"Yes. We had to leave the kuttub early. The funeral was brought forward."

"Oh?" said Georgiades, surprised. "Why was that?"

"I don't know. It was going to be later but then the fiki came in and told us we had to leave at once."

"Which is your kuttub?" asked Georgiades, with a sudden interest in his voice.

"It's in the fountain house."

"Near the Souk Al-Gadira?"

"That's right," said the boy. "Do you know it?"

"Very well," said Georgiades, looking at Owen. "Very well."

✺

"It is strange how the threads of our lives are intertwined," Owen said to Ali Marwash. "Do I not remember seeing your daughter's procession on the day she was first taken to the Place of Tombs? I was searching for those very guns at the time. It was near the Souk Al-Gadira."

He mentioned the date.

"Why, yes," said Ali Marwash, "that was the day. It may have been so."

"It was late in the morning, shortly before noon."

"That would be about right," Ali Marwash agreed.

"I remember it," said Owen, "because I was a little surprised. Was it not early for a funeral?"

"It was brought forward," said Ali, "by order of the Imam. Why, I don't know."

☙❧

"Hurry is the curse of the age," Owen said to the Imam, "and what does it profit us? We but hasten to our graves."

"True," said the Imam, much struck. "Very true."

"Take this poor girl, for instance. Was there any need to hurry her to the tomb? Might not the seed of all that later befell her lie in that very despatch? For surely God does not like the unseemly."

"*Was* she hurried to the tomb?" asked the Imam.

"Was not the funeral brought forward?"

"Was it? I don't remember."

"You did not order it to be brought forward?"

"No," said the Imam, "why should I do that? These things, as you properly remarked, should not be hurried. The funeral, I now remember, was indeed brought forward. But that was nothing to do with me. I was just told about it."

"Who told you?"

"The fiki, I think."

☙❧

"I knew I'd seen him before," said Georgiades. "It was when I was checking up at the kuttub. I saw him talking to the master."

"Nikos said there was a fiki there who was organizing things."

"Quite a lot of things. More than we thought."

"How did he do it? He would have had to move fast."

"Yes. He must have got the funeral procession on the road immediately he heard you were searching that area. Tacked a couple of spare donkeys on the back, I expect. Then, when he got to the school, he collected the arms—"

"How did he do that? Wouldn't the kids have seen him?"

"He probably sent them out to play. Anyway, he loaded up the donkeys and rejoined the procession—"

"I *saw* that procession. It passed just by us. Right under our noses!"

"—and went with it to the Place of Tombs. If the donkeys were at the back it would have been easy to drop them off somewhere and then go back for them."

"He wouldn't have had time. He had to go on to the house."

"It wouldn't have taken him long, though I agree he had to hurry. In fact, that probably explains it. Why he dumped the guns in the girl's tomb. He didn't have time to look for anywhere else. He probably just dropped behind and said he'd catch up. And then he had to work very fast."

"That might explain the body, too."

"Yes. He started putting the guns in and then he found there wasn't enough room. He had to choose between the guns and the girl. Well, the guns were important and the girl was only a girl—that's how he would see it—so out she came."

"He couldn't leave her, though."

"No, he had to get rid of her in a hurry. How he hit on that other tomb, I don't know. Perhaps he saw it had recently been disturbed and reckoned it would be quicker to get into. He didn't have much time."

"It was smart work."

"He's a smart bloke."

"Well, we've got him now. And with any luck we'll get his friends, too, and put a stop to arms smuggling for a year or two at least in this part of Cairo."

Georgiades grunted agreement. They walked on in silence for some way. Georgiades, however, was still thinking over Owen's remarks. "More than that, perhaps," he said, "more than that. We've been assuming he hit on the other tomb by accident. But suppose it wasn't accident? Suppose he knew about it already?"

Chapter 11

"Suppose he did?" Owen said to Mahmoud. "I don't see where that gets us."

"I do," said Mahmoud, springing to his feet. "I do."

They were sitting in a café outside the Law Courts. Although it was noon the café was three-quarters empty. Most other lawyers had finished for the day and gone home for their siesta.

Not Mahmoud, however. He never took a siesta and was always mildly surprised that the rest of the world could bear to take the time off work.

He didn't take lunch, either. They were merely drinking coffee.

It had been stiflingly hot in the Courts that morning and when he had come out to meet Owen his face had seemed lined with fatigue.

Now, however, he was pacing about excitedly, oblivious of the other patrons of the café, most of whom, admittedly, were lawyers and used to Mahmoud's eccentricities.

"I do," he said, almost jumping with pleasure.

He strode round the table and came face to face with Owen.

"Let me put a question to you," he said, bending towards him intently.

Owen flinched slightly. This was, he supposed, how Mahmoud carried on when he was examining witnesses in the courts.

"Go back to Leila's body. Found by those two beggars and hidden under a boat. Now let me ask you: who besides the beggars knew about that?"

"The boatman."

"And? Remember, the boatman was explicitly warned off. It was somebody else's business."

"The Man's?"

"Exactly. The beggars were carrying out instructions. It was their job to look after the first part of the operation only. After that it was up to someone else. Someone who was going to undertake the second part of the operation: transferring the body to a more secure hiding place."

"You think that—?"

Mahmoud laid a finger on his lips. He wasn't having his cross-examination disrupted by an unruly witness.

"Now let us look at it from another point of view. Leila's body turns up in the tomb. Who—who do we *know*—knew about the existence of the tomb?"

"Well, the fiki. But—"

Mahmoud's hand waved him firmly down.

"All we *know*," he said, cautioning Owen to mental discipline, "all we *know* is that from the time of the Marwash girl's funeral he knew about the tomb. We know, because he put the Marwash girl's body there."

"Strictly speaking," said Owen—he could play this game too—"we don't know that. We are just assuming that the fiki stage-managed the whole thing."

Mahmoud's hand dismissed this.

"I think we can accept Georgiade's arguments. I agree with him. He had to get rid of the body in a hurry. What more likely than that he would turn to a place he already knew?"

"He knew because he had already used it previously—to hide Leila's body in."

"Correct!" snapped Mahmoud triumphantly. He stood for a moment, thinking.

"There are other possible connections here," he said, frowning. He looked at Owen. "One of them you may be particularly interested in following up. If the fiki is connected with the arms trade and also with the Man, then perhaps the Man is connected with the arms trade."

Owen sat up.

"The Man is behind it?"

"Taking a cut, more likely," said Mahmoud, "as he does in most of the business along the river."

He was not, however, really thinking about that. That part of it he had, as it were, sectioned off and handed to Owen. It was the other parts that now engaged him.

"The problem for us all along," he said, brow furrowed, "has been the way in which the killing was carried out. It was essential to find the body because otherwise we couldn't be sure. Well, we're sure now. She was garotted. Now garotting, properly done as this was, requires a professional. Tell me," he said, looking at Owen—resuming, in fact, his cross-examination—"if you wanted a professional garotter in Cairo, how would you go about finding one?"

"I'd go to someone who could hire me one."

"Someone like—?"

"The Man. Are you suggesting—?"

"Why not?" Mahmoud sprang out of his chair again, blazing. "Why not?" he said. "It would make sense. It all hangs together. Disposing of the body might just have been part of it. We know the Man was involved with picking up the body and hiding it. Why shouldn't he be involved with the rest of it as well?"

"Providing the garotter—?"

"Yes. Providing the garotter, disposing of the body—And that would explain why it took place where it did. It's all in the Man's territory. Where he has things under control, where he can lay on people. A garotter, beggars, a local middleman like the fiki—"

"Will he talk?" said Owen.

"He?"

"The fiki."

"He might. He might."

"If he did," said Owen, "you could get the Man."

Mahmoud now was irrepressible.

"We'll get him," he said. "We'll get him."

"There is another thing, too," said Owen, watching him in his perambulations. "It could explain the garotter. No one had seen him on board. Because he never was on board. He came out from the shore, killed her and then went back. He was a local man."

Mahmoud stopped, transfixed.

"Yes," he breathed. "And to do that he would have had to have known where the dahabeeyah was going to moor for the night."

"Which means that it would have had to have been planned beforehand."

"Yes," said Mahmoud exultantly.

"Who decides where they're going to moor for the night?"

"Who gives the orders on the dahabeeyah?"

"The Rais?"

"Try again," said Mahmoud.

"Narouz."

☙❧

"Who took the decision? The Rais, I suppose."

"He says the itinerary was mapped out ahead at the start of the journey."

"So it was, now I come to think of it," said Prince Narouz. "But is that important?"

"Yes. It affects where the dahabeeyah was moored on the night Leila Sekhmet was killed."

"And that matters?"

"We think so," said Owen.

The Prince shrugged and looked at his watch.

"So I wonder if you could tell me," said Owen, "what made you decide to moor there that night?"

"We were going to put the girls ashore there. I thought it would be less conspicuous than having them travel on with us to Bulak. It was, after all, roughly where we picked them up."

"You didn't want people to know you'd had them on board?"

"My dear friend," said Narouz wearily, "of course not."

"You could have landed them that night."

"So I could. But I did not."

"Why not?"

"Your questions," said Narouz, "are beginning to border on the impertinent. However, I will tell you. I had hoped to prolong the pleasure of our voyage by one further day. And one further night, of course. I hope I make my meaning plain, even to a Mamur Zapt who appears to be at his obtusest this morning."

"The girls knew about the arrangement, did they? You had spoken to them about it?"

"I really cannot recall. They certainly knew I did not intend to sail up and down that confounded river like the Flying Dutchman until the crack of doom. Two weeks is more than enough."

"Yet you wished to prolong it."

"You take me up," said Narouz, "on trivialities. I am beginning to resent this cross-examination."

"The issues are important, Prince."

"I don't think they are." Prince Narouz stood up abruptly. "I don't think they're important at all. I see no point in continuing this tedious conversation."

⌛

Owen had just got back in his office when the phone rang. It was his friend Paul from the Consulate-General.

"Hello, Gareth. This is an Official Warning. Well, not very official, actually, but definitely a warning. The CG says will you lay off Narouz. The Khedive has just been on to him. He says you've been harassing Narouz. Now, would a nice chap like you do a thing like that? Yes. I know you would. So please don't. I thought you were supposed to be playing this down?"

"I am. But it's getting increasingly difficult. I told you about that bit in *Al-Liwa*, didn't I?"

"I thought you'd cut it out?"

"I did. But it's started coming out in other papers now. Illicit ones."

"Can't you do something about that?"

"Harass them, you mean?"

Paul breathed heavily. "Just keep the publicity down, will you? The Talks are at a delicate stage."

"They always are."

"No, they really are, this time. Two more days and we may have got it."

"The Agreement? Wouldn't it have to be ratified?"

"It would be better if it was ratified. But we could manage without it. The Khedive's an Absolute Ruler, well, relatively Absolute, and can conduct Agreements on his own, provided we say so. So we don't want him being upset by you doing the heavy stuff on Narouz."

"I'll try not to. But look, we're not going to be able to keep this quiet for very much longer. Even the news that an Agreement is on the cards is out in the radical press."

"Jesus!" said Paul. "Look, try and keep it down, will you? Just to the end of the week. That may well be enough."

ᏇᎲᎲᏇ

It was, however, easier said than done.

Nikos had had no difficulty in identifying the printer responsible for the radical pamphlet attacking Narouz and giving details of the incident on the dahabeeyah. He maintained a list of printers in the city, together with examples of their work. Provided the press was known, he reckoned to be able to attribute matter to printer within minutes.

Because of the investment required, sizable in Egyptian terms even for a small press, most presses were known and it had not taken him long to trace the pamphlet to a particular printer who specialized in the production of radical material.

What was much more difficult, however, was to establish the present whereabouts of the printer. Those who dealt in radical material moved often.

Nikos, though, was an old hand at this game and shortly after Paul's telephone call he entered Owen's office triumphantly brandishing a slip of paper.

"I had their distributors followed! They're not even bothering to use a different collection point. They pick it up straight from the press. I suppose," he said, "they're so keen to get it out."

"Yes," said Owen sourly. "They would be."

He picked up the piece of paper with the address.

"Why!" he said in surprise. "It's in Al-Gadira!"

"Yes," said Nikos, "the souk. It should be easy to find."

It took them a little time, in fact, because it was tucked away in a side street and in the back room of a shop. The front was occupied by a small tailor's.

Owen, accustomed to such raids, had brought with him both uniformed and, well, not exactly plainclothes, rather, undressed men. The constables were for breaking in should the premises be barred. They liked breaking into places. The undressed were for exactly such exigencies as this.

They sauntered along the street beforehand trying to spot the place. Failing to spot it, they began to make discreet inquiries. However discreet, inquiries were inquiries and it would be only a very short time before the printer got wind of them.

Fortunately, a man was seen emerging from the tailor's shop carrying a bundle of pamphlets. He was, wisely, not approached but allowed to proceed to the end of the street where Owen's uniformed detachment was waiting, pretending to be interested in some quite other establishment, to the anxiety of its proprietor.

The constables arrested him. They liked that sort of thing, too.

Owen sent his undressed men to the rear of the shop and then marched quickly along the street with his constables.

They took the tailor by surprise. He had not time to warn the inner room. Owen went straight on through.

Inside was a man in a skullcap working a press. On the floor roundabout were piles of the illicit pamphlets.

"Yours?" asked Owen, showing the man one of the pamphlets.

The man shrugged and folded his arms, waiting for the inevitable.

The constables began to carry out the confiscated material.

Owen went through a rear door and called in his other men. They set to work dismantling the press. It was the loss of the font that was irreparable. That, for a printer, was the real punishment. A spell in prison was neither here nor there, a mere occupational hazard.

There was a small table beyond the press, on which were several sheets of handwritten material. Owen glanced through them. They appeared to be copy for the next number: radical, but not, so far as Owen could see on a cursory glance, touching on the Leila affair.

"Where do you put your old copy?" he asked the printer.

The printer shrugged and remained mute.

There were some big wicker baskets by the door, which served as dustbins. Owen tipped their contents out onto the floor and began to go through them carefully.

He found the copy for the Narouz number. It consisted of several carefully handwritten sheets in Arabic. He smoothed them out to make sure.

"Who brought you this?" he asked the printer.

The printer did not even bother to shrug.

Owen didn't waste any more time on him but went immediately into the front room of the shop where one of his constables had the tailor pinioned against the wall.

"Your name?" he said to the tailor.

"Abdul Hamid."

"Do I know you, Abdul Hamid? Have you been in trouble before?"

"No," said the man.

"I hope that is true. Do you own this shop?"

"Yes, effendi."

"You know, then, to whom you have let it. You know what he publishes. You are, therefore, held responsible under the law."

"Yes, effendi," said the man sadly.

"The minimum punishment is a heavy fine."

"I cannot pay a fine, effendi," said the tailor. "Look around you."

It was indeed a poor man's shop.

"Then you will have to go to prison."

"So be it." The man's shoulders drooped.

"I can make it lighter," said Owen, "but for that I should need something in return."

"Alas," said the tailor, showing the palms of his hands, "I have nothing to give."

"It is not money I want," said Owen. "It is your memory."

"My memory?" said the tailor, surprised.

"I need to know about the men who have visited this place."

"Effendi," said the man hesitantly, "I would help you. I have no wish to go to prison. I do not own this shop, I rent it, and if I went to prison I would not be able to keep up with the payments. I would lose all I have. I will help you if I can. But, effendi, there have been so many people coming and going, especially in the last few days, that I cannot remember them all."

"No matter. If you do your best, that is enough. Go with this man"—he indicated one of the plainclothes men—"the Bab el Khalk. As for Nikos. Tell him all you know. And I shall be content."

The tailor bowed his head in acknowledgment and left the room with the plainclothes man.

Owen waited until the room had been cleared. As the last pamphlets were being removed, one of the policemen said:

"We've got this lot, anyway."

"It's too late," said Owen, slipping the handwritten copy into his pocket, "they're all over the place already."

They were. Zeinab handed him a copy when he went to her flat that evening.

"Read it," she said with satisfaction.

"I have already," he said, handing it back. "Where did you get hold of that?"

"Hargazy gave it me," she said.

"Hargazy?"

"That friend of Gamal's who knew Leila. We met him after the play, remember. The one who probably wrote that article for *Al-Liwa*."

"Yes, I remember. Hates us."

"He doesn't hate you particularly," said Zeinab. "Or the British. It's Narouz he hates, Narouz, the Khedive, the whole lot of them."

"The Pashas? Your father?"

"My father is different."

"You're different, too, evidently. He doesn't hate you."

"I told him I would help him. To tell the world about Leila."

"And this is part of it, is it?" said Owen, looking at the pamphlet she still held in her hand. "Telling the world?"

"It's a good start," said Zeinab with satisfaction.

"Do you know how I have been spending the morning? I've been raiding the printer who produced this."

"You're a confused man," said Zeinab, "who doesn't know right from wrong."

"Closed him down, too. He won't be producing any more of this sort of stuff for a while," he said, tapping the pamphlet with his finger.

Zeinab got herself up on the divan, curled her legs up under her, and began to smolder.

"If you wish to be my enemy," she said, "so be it."

"I don't wish to be your enemy. I am as anxious as you are to see whoever killed Leila caught."

"In that case," said Zeinab, "why don't you arrest Narouz?"

"Because—" said Owen, and stopped.

He had been about to say that the evidence was as yet insufficient, that there was still room for doubt, that until a person was proved guilty he must be treated as innocent. But then he stopped.

"Because?" asked Zeinab.

"Because it's—it's not yet the right moment," he finished lamely.

"I know why it's not the right moment," said Zeinab, gathering in fury. "It's because of this Secret Agreement of yours. Secret Agreement, pah! Which everybody knows about and has been the talk of the bazaars for weeks! Even my hair-dresser knows that the Agreement is to be signed on Friday. Friday! The Moslem sabbath! That is a fine day to sign an Agreement on! If that doesn't bring people onto the streets, nothing will."

She paused to draw breath.

"The Agreement is a consideration, I admit—"

"'Consideration?' What are these men's words when a woman lies dead?"

"But not the only one, of course."

"No? I am glad to hear it. For I thought for a moment that it was. And if it was, then let me tell you that you are making a great mistake. For if the people are angry because an injustice has been done, then it is no use making Agreements."

"We don't know that an injustice has been done," said Owen.

"*I* know," said Zeinab, "and when I have finished, everyone else will know, too."

Owen, wisely, kept quiet.

"You can arrest me if you like," said Zeinab defiantly.

"Good idea!" snapped Owen, and moved onto the divan beside her.

"Keep your hands off!" shouted Zeinab, convinced for the moment that he intended to.

Then—

"Keep your hands off!" she shouted, as she became convinced otherwise.

Owen pulled back, slid down on to the floor and sat comfortably on a cushion at Zeinab's feet. After a moment he felt Zeinab's hand ruffling his hair.

"It's no good," she said calmly, "it'll be in all the papers now."

"Oh, I know that."

"Hargazy has contacts everywhere. He's been working night and day."

"Has he? Why is it so important to him?"

Zeinab withdrew her hand.

"Because he loved Leila. He is not," she said pointedly, "like some men."

ᑐᙏᙢᑐ

He found Gamal in his usual café. It was early in the morning and the playwright's friends had not yet arrived. He was at his usual table, bent over, writing. This was where he did his work.

He looked up vaguely and caught Owen's eye. Immediately, he dropped his pen and jumped up.

"My friend! *Mon très, très cher ami!*"

"Gamal!"

They embraced.

"*Un apéritif?*"

"*Permettez-moi!*"

They settled down and Gamal pushed his writing pad away.

"It's all right," he said, "I've finished for the day. It wasn't going well, anyway."

Owen asked after Gamal's plays. Gamal shrugged.

"Next time, perhaps," he said.

He asked what Owen was doing.

"Still working on the Leila business."

Gamal looked sad.

"That was bad," he said. "It did not show us in a good light, did it? I have been thinking about it. We did not care, my friend, we did not care enough. She was one of us and we know she was troubled and not one of us thought fit to ask her about herself. That was bad, my friend, that was bad."

"Was she really one of you?"

"Well…" Gamal hesitated. "Not really. But that again is not good. Was the reason that she was not really one of us the fact that she was a woman? I ask myself this, my friend. Would it have been different in France? I ask myself."

"You were the only people she could come to," Owen pointed out, "the only ones who would have her."

Gamal was pleased at this.

"Yes," he said, "you are right. We artists have our faults but social narrowness is not among them."

"It was a pity she did not stay with Suleiman."

Gamal shook his head.

"He was working on something. It was a big commission and he was worried about it. That, I am afraid, *is* one of our faults. When we are working on something we become preoccupied with it. It takes us over. There is no space for anything. There was no space for Leila."

"So she took up with Hargazy."

Gamal pursed his lips.

"Hargazy was not the right man for her."

"Too bitter?"

Gamal looked at him in surprise.

"Yes," he said, "you are right. He *is* bitter. But that is not why he was the wrong man for her. He did not love her. She was a plaything, a toy. Something to be used, then cast aside. It could not last."

Owen remembered something Prince Fahid had said.

"You think that it might have already ended by the time she was taken up by Narouz? That that was one of the reasons why she agreed to go with him on the dahabeeyah?"

"Perhaps," said Gamal. "Who knows?"

An agitated phone call from Mahmoud.

"Have you heard?"

"Heard what?"

"Narouz has gone."

"What do you mean—'gone'?"

"Left the country."

"Left the country?"

"You haven't heard? He was supposed to turn up at a meeting this morning. It's to do with that Agreement they're signing. Anyway, he didn't arrive. The Khedive wanted to know why. Somebody said he'd left the country."

"Rumor!" said Owen.

"Yes, but he wasn't there this morning."

"I'll check."

He went to the Prince's *appartement*.

"I am afraid, effendi, that His Highness is not at home," said the servant politely.

"Does that mean he will be in later?"

The servant hesitated. But he had seen Owen at the Prince's house before, his relations with Narouz were, as far as he knew, friendly, and, besides, Owen was an English effendi.

"I don't think so, effendi," he said reluctantly.

"Have you any idea where he's gone?"

"I am afraid not, effendi."

"His estate, perhaps?"

"I don't think so, effendi," said the servant, certain of that at least.

"Cannes, more likely," said Nikos, picking up the phone.

"What are you doing?"

"Checking boats."

There was one leaving Alexandria the following day.

"How do you know it's Alexandria and not Port Said?"

"Well," said Nikos, "what do you think?"

Port Said traffic went to India.

"He's not that desperate," said Nikos.

"All right, it's Alexandria. But there'll be other boats besides that one tomorrow."

"Two a week go to France. The other one left three days ago."

"He might have gone to Turkey."

"Narouz?"

The Egyptian road system remained in a fortunate state of underdevelopment. There was only one road going to Alexandria from Cairo and cars, as opposed to bullocks and donkeys and camels, were so infrequent as to be remarkable. More remarkable still was a touring model painted vivid green. The reports soon came in.

"Oh yes, effendi," said the peculiarly dreamy policeman at the station on the Alexandria Road, "it flashed by me yesterday evening."

Admittedly, anything would flash by that particular observer but more reliable accounts came in from other points along the road: places where the drovers watered their camels, where the bullock drivers had their tea.

Above all, the petrol stations, of which there were two between Cairo and Alexandria. They were not properly service stations, of course—the traffic did not justify it—but depots for Army vehicles, whose services were commissioned by the Prince on the grounds that as nephew to the Khedive he was nearly Commander-in-Chief.

The Prince would have reached Alexandria that morning. Nikos anticipated no difficulty in locating him.

"He's not going to be staying in some flea-ridden place, is he? We'll find him at the Windsor. The question is: What are you going to do then?"

☙❧

"Yes," said Paul, "I had heard. Does it matter?"

"Of course it matters. He'll catch the next boat out of Alexandria."

"So?"

"He'll get away."

"He's a free man. He can go where he likes. He's not been charged with anything."

"That's what I'm talking about."

"Charging him? Is that something for you to do? Surely not. You're always telling me that ordinary crime is no business of the Mamur Zapt. This is ordinary crime, isn't it? Leave it to Mahmoud."

"He thinks it political."

"Because we're talking about a relative of the Khedive? It may be political in his terms but it's not in ours, surely? Purely Egyptian matter. Leave it to Mahmoud."

"He won't be able to get it through."

"Then should we help him? That *would* make it political, wouldn't it, interfering with the Khedive's direction of his own Ministries?"

"Paul, this is political in *our* terms, too. It's going to be all over the town, and people are not going to like it. They're not going to like the Khedive, either. And how do you think they're going to feel about any Agreement he signs?"

"Mutinous, I'd say. Fortunately we have a Mamur Zapt to look after that kind of thing. Privately, Gareth, I'm inclined to agree with you. Publicly, though, I have to tell you we're so far down the road with this damned Agreement that we can't let anything stop it now. It's being signed on Friday."

"Yes, I know. And that's another thing. Friday! Hasn't it occurred to anyone that Friday is a special day to Moslems? Couldn't you make it another day?"

"Lord, I'd forgotten that! It's being signed by some bigwig and he wanted to be on his way to London by the weekend. Still, I'll pass it on to the CG. Well spotted, Gareth! That's the kind of thing we pay you for. Why don't you concentrate on that sort of activity for the next day or two?"

ᏰᎷᏬ

By noon even Zeinab's hairdresser had heard about it.

"What are you going to do?" asked Zeinab.

Chapter 12

"Mr. Hargazy," said Owen, "I wonder if you can tell me something about the authorship of this article?"

He handed him the pamphlet containing the attack on Narouz.

"It's the one on the front page."

Hargazy glanced at it, then handed it back.

"Well written, I would say. A cut above the usual rubbish."

"Well informed, too?"

"It seems to be."

"A trifle intemperate in tone, don't you think?"

"No. I wouldn't say that. Given the subject."

"Of course, Leila Sekhmet was known to you, wasn't she?"

"And to many others, yes. She wasn't especially close to me."

"Really? I thought you were very close."

"I slept with her, if that's what you mean. But that does not make her close."

"You surprise me. I had formed the impression you cared for her deeply."

"You are thinking of the conversation I had with Zeinab? I care about the fact of her death. I care, deeply, about her as an example of the way our country is oppressed by those who rule her. As a symbol, that is, I care for her. But as a person? I would not say she mattered to me very much as a person."

"And yet you have busied yourself very much on her behalf," Owen pointed out.

"The symbol is important to me. Our country is a big country, Captain Owen, and it needs something to focus its anger and indignation. The only way I can see that happening is through an individual case which somehow takes on representative qualities, becomes, as I say, a symbol."

"And that is what Leila Sekhmet means to you?"

"Exactly."

Hargazy, tieless but jacketed, seemed very much at ease.

"You are, of course, an artist," said Owen, "and like to deal in the symbolic."

"Well..." Hargazy looked deprecatingly at his shoes.

Owen went through the papers on his desk.

"As well as this article, you wrote the other one, didn't you, the one that appeared in *Al-Liwa*?"

"Was to have appeared." Hargazy smiled. "I believe you were the one who censored it out?"

"But you were the author?"

"I did not say that."

"No. I'm saying that."

"On what basis?"

"Handwriting. I have the original copy for the article which appeared in the pamphlet. It's in your handwriting."

"Well," said Hargazy, "it's hardly worth bothering, is it? You're going to hold me anyway, aren't you?"

"Yes."

"For how long?"

"Certainly for the next few days."

"Until the Agreement is signed?"

"Yes."

Hargazy seemed relaxed about it.

"It's not important now, anyway," he said. "The news is out. Stories have a momentum of their own."

"I think you'll find that momentum can be arrested."

"You won't be able to seize *all* the copies," Hargazy said confidently.

"I'll be able to seize enough of them. And then I'll introduce another story which will take over in the headlines."

There was a flicker of doubt. Then Hargazy recovered.

"It won't work," he said.

"Won't it? Is a woman that important in this country?"

"No, but Narouz is."

Owen shuffled through his papers again and found the scurrilous pamphlet.

"What have you got against Narouz?" he asked.

"He's one of *them*."

"Only that?"

"Isn't that enough?"

"Nothing to do with Leila?"

"Why do you keep asking me about Leila? She was something to use, that was all."

Owen looked at the pamphlet again. And at all the other pamphlets.

"Well," he said, "you've used her very successfully, I must admit. The story is everywhere."

Hargazy smiled.

Owen closed the file. The constable at the door stirred.

"Before you go," said Owen, "there's one other thing. I'm trying to find who killed Leila and you might be able to help me. Where did you get your story from?"

"I'm a journalist," said Hargazy. "I don't reveal my sources."

∽

"So you've clamped down?" said Garvin.

Owen nodded.

"We're picking up anybody distributing illegal material."

"The Ataba will be quiet today," said Garvin, amused.

"It won't last, of course. They'll be back on the streets tomorrow."

"That might be just long enough. Good," said Garvin. "Very good."

Nikos stuck his head in at the door.

"There's someone to see you."

"Who is it?"

"He says he's a watchman. A ghaffir."

"A ghaffir? What does he want?"

"I don't know. All he'll say is that he's from the Souk Al-Gadira."

"Ah. In that case, show him in."

In came a nervous-looking Arab who seemed familiar.

"It is Abu, effendi," he said hesitantly.

"Abu?"

"You saw me down by the river, effendi. I was the one who found the girl."

"Ah yes. I remember you, Abu."

"Effendi, I have something terrible to tell you."

He plucked at his galabeah nervously.

"You have? What is it, Abu?"

The watchman tried to speak but the words would not come.

"Do not be afraid, Abu, I know that you are a good man."

The words suddenly came with a rush.

"Effendi, they tricked me! That Ibrahim! And I thought he was such a nice man! A corporal, too!"

"How exactly did he trick you, Abu?"

"That morning, effendi. That morning when I found the body. I went to the Chief and he told me to go back and show Ibrahim the body, that he might mount guard on it. But that false Ibrahim, on the way there he sent me away and while I was away—oh, effendi, you will not believe this— he took a pole and thrust the body off the sandbank. Then, when I came back, he pretended to know nothing. And I—I— the effendi came, and what could I say? The body wasn't there."

"I see. And you have just found out about all this?"

"Yes, effendi. And then I could not rest. For, I said, the effendi has been beguiled, and who knows what may befall?

And then I thought: Abu, you must tell him. But I did not want to, effendi, because the Bab el Khalk is a great distance and you are a great man. And I may be beaten for my simplicity. But then, effendi, I thought: Abu, you are a ghaffir and it is your duty. And so, effendi, I have come."

He came to a halt, breathless, and stood, diffident and apologetic, his eyes fixed earnestly on Owen.

Owen, at bottom another simple man, and moreover, Welsh, with all a Welshman's emotional responsiveness, was touched. He came out from behind his desk and put his arm round Abu.

"You are a good man, Abu. Did I not say so, and have you not shown yourself so to be?"

"You are not going to beat me?" said Abu, a little surprised.

"Certainly not."

"The Chief will."

"No, he won't," said Owen. "Not after I've had a word with him. Besides," he added, stepping back, "all this is known already."

Abu's jaw dropped.

"Known already?"

"Yes. I've known it for some time."

Abu pulled himself together. He shook his head in wonderment.

"The Mamur Zapt knows all," he said, impressed.

"Not quite all."

Abu fidgeted.

"Then, then—there was no point in my coming?"

"You did right, Abu, and did your duty. Every man should do his duty," said Owen sententiously, giving himself a mental kick.

Abu looked pleased.

"And it does not matter, effendi?"

"Not now, no. You see, when Ibrahim went to push the body off with his pole, he found it had already gone. He—"

"Gone!" said Abu, thunderstruck anew.

"Yes, and we know how it went. Two beggars—I expect they are known to you, their names are Libab and Farag—"

"But I know them!" said Abu excitedly.

"Yes, they always work that stretch of the bank. Anyway, they found the body and hid it under a boat."

"Farag and Libab! I saw them there that morning!"

"Yes."

A thought suddenly struck him.

"Abu, did you see anyone else that morning? You see, the body was hidden under a boat nearby and later in the day someone came to fetch it."

Abu shook his head.

"I saw no one with a body," he said.

"Perhaps not with a body. That is not to be expected. It would have been moved by night. But someone down there. Perhaps talking to the boatman."

"I saw many people," said Abu, shaking his head.

"Did you, perhaps, see a fiki?"

"Why, yes," said Abu, "I did."

⧉

This early in the morning there was still a tinge of freshness in the air, especially so close to the river. Some storks were wading in the shallows. They moved a little further out as Owen and Mahmoud approached but did not fly away.

A little beyond them the boatman was already at work. A small brazier was burning and from it came the pungent smell of boiling tar.

The boatman looked up as they arrived. He recognized Mahmoud but not Owen.

"Effendi," he said politely.

"Greetings, Mohammed Farkas," said Mahmoud. He went and stood among the boats drawn up on the bank. "Remind me, Mohammed Farkas," he said, "which boat was the girl's body hidden under?"

The boatman's face fell.

"This one, effendi." He indicated it with his hand.

"Ah, you've moved it."

"It has been on the water, effendi."

"Yes, of course."

Mahmoud sat down on the upturned hull.

"This is my friend," he said, indicating Owen. "He is the Mamur Zapt."

"I have told you all I know, effendi," said the boatman in a low voice.

"Not quite all, I think."

"What else is it you wish to know, effendi?"

"You told me that after the beggars had spoken to you, you did not go near the boat because you were afraid. And that when you next looked under the boat, two days later, the body was gone."

"That is true, effendi."

"Well, yes, but not the whole truth."

The boatman was silent.

"Tell me, for instance: when did the fiki come?"

"Fiki?" said the boatman, swallowing.

"We could fetch him if you liked. But will that be necessary?"

"No, effendi," said the boatman sadly.

"When, then?"

"In the afternoon, effendi."

"He surely did not take the body then?"

"He came to see that it was there. Then he came again in the night."

"You saw him?"

"Effendi, I—I was sleeping."

"Where were you sleeping?"

The boatman indicated one of the boats.

"There? Then I think you saw him. Did you not see him, Mohammed Farkas?"

"Yes, effendi," the boatman said reluctantly.

"Did he speak to you?"

"No, effendi." The boatman gathered up courage. "And I did not speak to him."

"The less you knew about it, the better? That was it, was it?"

"Yes, effendi."

"Well, that was wise of you. And now you are going to be wiser still. For the Mamur Zapt is right beside you. He has heard what you have said, so when I ask you about the fiki again, in the Great Court, you will repeat what you have said and not pretend you did not say it."

The boatman went pale.

"Effendi," he pleaded, "he will have me killed."

"The fiki? I do not think so."

"No, not the fiki."

"Who, then?"

෨෩

Owen had to hurry back to the Bab el Khalk. He had barely settled himself in his chair when Nikos stuck his head in.

"Someone else to see you," he said. "You're popular today. Though I don't think it will last. Prince Narouz."

"Prince Narouz!" Owen leaped to his feet and hurried to the door, hand outstretched in greeting. "What a relief to see you!"

"Relief?" said Narouz, taken aback.

"I feared—Your Highness, do sit down! I am afraid my office is a little spartan. This chair, for instance—" Owen shook his hand. Then, seeing a goggle-eyed Nikos still at the door: "Coffee! Coffee for His Highness!"

"Coffee!" snapped Nikos, pulling himself together. He disappeared down the corridor. They heard his voice in the distance. "Coffee!"

"Coffee?" said Narouz, bewildered.

Owen took him by the arm, held him at arm's length and inspected him affectionately.

"You're all right!" he said fervently.

"Of course I'm all right. Why shouldn't I be?"

Owen shook his hand as if he could hardly believe his eyes.

"You're safe!" he said. "That's the main thing. Your well-being, Prince, must always be my highest consideration."

"Well, thank you," said the Prince. "I am, naturally, gratified. But why exactly—?"

Owen returned to his desk and sat down.

"We should have warned you before, Your Highness. I realize that now. We have been watching them for weeks. But we did not wish to alarm you unnecessarily and it was only yesterday that it became clear."

"*What* became clear?"

"That you were to be the target."

"Target!"

"And then we heard of your sudden call to Alexandria! I don't mind telling you, Prince, now, that for a moment I was in despair. I had to act quickly. Not too quickly, I hope?" he said, smiling solicitously.

"I thought for a moment," said the Prince slightly diffidently, "that I was being—well, arrested."

"Oh, Prince!" said Owen, shocked. "Surely not!"

"Well, they said I was being held."

"Held safe. Guarded. Protected," Owen assured him.

"Well…" The Prince was silent for a moment. "And what, exactly," he added, "am I being protected from?"

"A terrorist group. We have had our eye on them for some time. But it's only recently that we have begun to suspect…It's the Agreement, you see. A last, desperate attempt to stop it being signed."

"The Agreement? But I'm nothing to do with that."

"But, Prince, you are! You've been party to the discussions, you've attended the sessions—"

"Only some of them. And, anyway, I'm only there to make up the numbers on the Khedive's side. He doesn't trust anyone else—"

"Well, there you are!" said Owen. "His right-hand man."

"But—"

"Heir to the throne. What better means of offering a dreadful, horrible warning to the Khedive?"

"Are you sure?"

"It's been building up," said Owen. "We should have spotted it. Your name—"

"My *name?*"

"You've seen the newspapers?"

"Yes, but—"

"The radical pamphlets? The illicit handbills?"

"Yes, but—"

"Your name," said Owen, "everywhere!"

"But surely—"

"You have become identified—in the popular mind—with all that is widely hated in Egypt at the present time, a symbol"—where had he heard this before?—"of all that the revolutionary movement is fighting against."

"My God!" said the Prince. "Have I?"

"It will blow over. It will take a day or two, a week or two, perhaps, but it will blow over. But meanwhile, for the sake of your own safety—"

"I'll leave at once," said the Prince. "I'll catch the next boat."

"No! Too dangerous!" said Owen hastily. "For the next few days it's absolutely vital that you stay where we can protect you."

"Army Headquarters?"

"I think your own house would do. It will be heavily guarded, I assure you. The one thing, though, that I absolutely insist on is that *you must not go out.*"

"You don't think France would be better?"

"We couldn't guard you. No, Prince, you're safer under our direct protection. In a few days it will all be over."

"Well," said the Prince doubtfully, "if you really think so."

"I do. And now it remains for us to make sure that you get home safely, I have ordered an escort—"

"Oh, good," said the Prince.

"Mounted."

"Mounted? On camels? But—"

"There will be guards traveling in your car. Heavily armed guards. You need have no fear."

"I am not so sure about that," said Narouz.

༻✦༺

For some time Owen had been observing—from a safe distance—the rump of a particularly large, mangy and clearly flea-ridden camel. He stirred restlessly.

"Why," he asked Georgiades, "have you brought me here?"

"Because," said Georgiades in injured tones, "this is where it all starts."

Owen looked round. They were in a large open compound on the edge of the town, just where the quarter gave onto the desert. Scattered around the compound were some two dozen camels, all hobbled by the knees in the desert way. And over beside a wall was a row of about a dozen donkeys, their tails flicking continuously at the flies.

"Here?"

"Here. It was, in fact," said Georgiades, "the donkeys that gave me the idea."

"I don't remember any donkeys," said Owen cautiously.

"I suggested, if you remember, that what the fiki may have done was to tack a couple of donkeys on the back of the funeral procession and use them to pick up the arms from the kuttub. Well, I checked up on that. And that," said Georgiades, "brought me here."

"He picked up the donkeys from here?"

"He picked up the whole funeral procession from here. The fiki has the name in the neighborhood of being a great fixer. If you want anything arranged, be it a wedding or a funeral, a house move or just your latrines emptied, you go to him. And he comes here."

"He comes here?" said Owen, surprised. Animals, in Egypt, represented capital, and there was a lot of capital here for a humble fiki.

"No. It belongs to a big camel contractor. Camels are his main business. The donkeys are just a sideline. The fiki, though, is his local man-on-the-spot. That is, for his less legitimate business."

At the far end of the compound some men were sitting on the ground around a brazier drinking tea. Two of them stood up and began to saunter across towards them. Georgiades pulled Owen back into the doorway.

"What is his less legitimate business?" asked Owen.

"Let me tell you about his legitimate business first. He buys camels in Syria and Palestine and then has them driven across the desert to the Canal. He picks them up at Kantara and then brings them here, where he sells them off."

"For food?"

Camel meat took the place of beef for the poorer Egyptian.

"Yes. That is his legitimate business. But it doesn't take much imagination to see that if you are regularly bringing camels into the country and across to Cairo, you can also bring other things."

"Such as arms?"

"And hashish. They put the hashish in little cylinders which they get the camels to swallow. Then when they slaughter them they extricate the cylinders."

"So the slaughters are part of it?"

"Yes, and the fiki another part. He arranges for the distribution once they get here. You see," said Georgiades, "that was another thing that struck me. Distribution. Even small parcels of arms are heavy. They've got to be carried. Donkeys are the obvious way of carrying them. And that brings us back to here. Donkeys are the clue to it all."

The two men had reached the camels now and were checking their saddlebags.

"So the fiki gets the arms here," said Owen, "and then distributes them by donkey. Does he distribute the hashish too?"

"The lot. He's into most things round here."

"And do you know who he distributes them to?"

"That's what has taken the time," said Georgiades. "I had to find a driver I could bribe."

"But you've found one?"

"Yes. It cost a lot." Georgiades gave Owen a sideways glance. "You're going to have to square this with Accounts."

Owen winced.

"It's audit," he said. "They send someone over from England. He doesn't always understand the way we do things here."

"It's in a good cause. Anyway, I got a lot of information from him, but of course he didn't do all the deliveries himself so it took him a bit of time to find out the other ones. However"—Georgiades tapped his pocket—"I have now got a list."

The two men, having checked the saddlebags, walked away again.

"Let me have a look."

"It's just deliveries. They might be arms, they might be hashish or they might be anything else. Even ordinary things like pianos. But mostly its fringe illicit. Radical literature, for example."

"Pamphlets?"

"And handbills. The lot. Anything bulky that has to be transported around the place." Georgiades dropped his voice to a confidential whisper. "Let me give you some advice. Arrest all the donkeys in town. That's the way to break the radical press."

"Thank you."

"Your friend Hargazy, for instance," said Georgiades.

"He uses these donkeys?"

"A lot."

"And the fiki organizes it for him?"

"For him and others. He's a busy man. As we have noticed."

He took the list out of his pocket and gave it to Owen.

"There's one on the back that will interest you."

Owen turned the page over.

"Narouz!"

"Narouz, question mark."

"Why 'question mark'?"

"Because I'm not sure he's in the same category as the others: someone being delivered something."

"Then why is he here?"

"The driver reports that one day he was delivering a load with the fiki and they met Narouz. It seemed to be by appointment. He mentioned it because he had been impressed."

"Where was this?"

"You'll be surprised."

The two men approached again. This time they unhobbled two of the camels and goaded them, protesting, to their feet. Then they took them by their lead ropes and headed out of the compound.

Georgiades watched them until they were halfway down the street and then touched Owen's arm.

"These ones we'll follow," he said.

As they threaded their way through the narrow streets, the people sitting in the shade of the open doorways did not give them a second glance. In this part of the city there were camels coming and going all the time, carrying wood, carrying water, carrying green fodder for the cab horses in the center of the town.

At this time of day, too, there were few people about. The sun was at its hottest and most people had retreated inside. The little stalls with their tomatoes and cucumbers and gherkins were deserted, apparently abandoned to whoever cared to pillage them. Only sometimes, underneath the stalls, in the shade, the owner was sleeping.

Following the soft pad of the camels along the sandy street, Owen could feel the sweat running off him. When it was so hot, the slightest motion set the moisture trickling.

They came to narrower, darker streets where the houses were high and kept out the sun. This was a residential area and there were few shops. The houses had their shutters closed. Everyone was indoors at their siesta.

They crossed a broader street which seemed vaguely familiar. Owen looked down it. At the far end it broadened out into a crossroads in which there seemed to be a large market.

"The souk?"

"Al-Gadira," said Georgiades.

The camels padded on.

And then, as the houses became smaller again and moved further apart, and the shade suddenly dwindled and they became conscious again of the oppression of the sun, they came to an open square.

The camels crossed the square and came to a stop outside a low building on the opposite side which Owen recognized at once.

The Police Station! The station he had come to on that first afternoon when all this business had started, the station from which he had first learned about the body on that sandbank.

"This is it," said Georgiades.

"It?"

"The place where the fiki met Narouz."

In the shade in front of the building a man was lying. He stood up as the camel drivers reached him. It was the corporal, Ibrahim, he of the pole. He saw the camels, went up the steps of the building and shouted to someone inside.

After a moment the District Chief emerged. He greeted the drivers and then walked over to the camels.

He stood for a moment looking and then bent down beside one of them. Owen saw him put his hand up under it and begin to palpate the animal's lower stomach.

The camel, never the most tractable of beasts, stood this for a moment and then began to sit. The Chief ducked nimbly out of the way and said something, smiling, to the camel drivers.

He moved on to the second camel. This was less tolerant and snatched its head back and tried to bite at him. The camel driver cursed and heaved its head round with the rope.

The camel then shied round and the Chief had to dodge swiftly out of the way of its hooves.

He seemed satisfied, however, and waved the camels on round to the rear of the building. Then he went back inside.

Owen followed him.

The Chief, who associated Owen with all that was bad, went pale.

Owen smiled.

"It was there all right, wasn't it? The hashish?"

The Chief went paler still.

"You have good friends, I see. Suppose you tell me about them?"

"What friends?" said the uncomfortable Chief, perspiring.

"The fiki, for a start."

Chapter 13

The fiki declined a chair and stood composed in the center of the room, his arms folded, looking down on Owen and Mahmoud.

It was late in the morning and the shutters had been closed against the sun. The only light was that which came through the slats of the shutters, so the room was in that strange state of half-light which was the normal light of interior Cairo.

"So you see," said Owen, "we know all about you. We know how the arms got here, we know how you distributed them, we know to whom they went."

"Why, then," asked the fiki, "do you wish to talk to me?"

"There are some other points we would like to clear up. Nothing to do with the arms. More, shall we say, incidental matters. We think you may be able to help us."

The fiki shrugged.

"The matter, for instance, of what happened to Leila Sekhmet's body."

"Sekhmet?"

"You don't know her name?"

"Why should I know her name?"

"I wondered if you did," said Owen. "That was all."

"No."

"Let me call her something else, then. The girl on the dahabeeyah. The one who was killed."

"What dahabeeyah was this?"

"The Prince's."

The fiki laughed. "I have nothing to do with princes," he said.

"No? And yet you have had something to do with this one. You met him, for instance. You see," said Owen, "we really do know all about you."

The fiki merely shrugged.

"The girl was garotted and her body thrown overboard. It came ashore on a sandbank, where it was found by two beggars, whose names I also know. They had been told to look out for it, because it was known that the body would be coming ashore. They had also been told what to do with it. Hide it nearby."

The fiki listened impassively.

"They hid it under a boat in a neighboring boatyard. Then, when it became dark, someone else picked it up."

"So?" said the fiki.

"The someone was you."

The fiki hesitated just a fraction of a second.

"So you say," he said.

"So I know. There was a witness. I also know," said Owen, "what happened after that. But perhaps you can tell me?"

"I do not think I can," said the fiki.

"No? Well, let me tell you. You took it to the Place of Tombs. And there you hid it. In a tomb that was known to you. Had you used it before, I wonder?"

The fiki watched Owen unblinkingly, like some great fat cat. He said nothing, however.

"You are still not going to help us? Well then, let us go on to the next bit. The occasion when you used it again."

"I did not use it before. So how could I use it again?"

"It was the occasion of the burial of Ali Marwash's daughter. That was a busy day indeed! You were, I expect, in the kuttub, hearing the boys' verses, when you learned that the Mamur Zapt was searching the area, was, perhaps, even then at the end of the street. You had to act quickly. The funeral procession was no doubt already gathering?"

"It was gathering," said the fiki, "and I was already with it."

"I do not think so. And nor do the boys in the kuttub."

"Boys!" said the fiki dismissively.

"They remembered that you had brought the funeral forward."

"I do not think it was brought forward."

"I do. And so do Ali Marwash and the Imam."

The fiki suddenly went still.

"You brought with you two donkeys," resumed Owen. "You filled their saddlebags with the arms from the kuttub. And then you rejoined the procession and went with it to the Place of Tombs."

"I went to the Place of Tombs, certainly," said the fiki.

"And there, afterwards, you hid the arms in the very tomb in which you had just placed Ali Marwash's daughter."

"So you say," muttered the fiki.

"So I know. And so soon will others. And when they do," said Owen quietly, "I do not think you will have many friends."

"Still fewer," said Mahmoud, speaking for the first time, "when they know that you were the one who thrust the girl's body unfeelingly into that other tomb, the tomb in which you had already placed Leila Sekhmet."

The fiki stood for some time with his head bowed. Then he raised his eyes.

"Since you know all these things," he said, "why do you ask me them?"

Mahmoud now took up the questioning.

"There are some things," he said, "which we would like to hear from your lips."

"Such as?"

"Who told you to collect Leila Sekhmet's body?"

"I cannot tell you that."

"As my friend has already told you, we know the answers to other questions. It was the Man, was it not?"

"I cannot tell you."

"Are you afraid? Afraid of what he might do?"

"I would be foolish if I were not afraid," said the fiki.

"You are going to prison anyway," said Owen. "You can tell us, for there you will be safe."

The fiki looked at him incredulously.

"Safe from the Man?" he said. "In prison?"

Mahmoud considered the point. Then he nodded his head gently, as if in agreement.

"Very well," he said. "Then tell me one other thing. And this you *can* tell us with safety. It is this. What did you talk about with the Prince Narouz?"

"With the Prince Narouz?" asked the fiki, surprised.

"We know you met him."

"Well, yes," said the fiki. "But surely..." He still seemed surprised. Then he shrugged his shoulders. "I offered him the girl's body," he said "The Chief had made it known that he would pay handsomely."

"And that was it?" asked Mahmoud skeptically.

"Yes," said the fiki. "What else could it be?"

"You tell me," said Mahmoud. "Or is this another of those things we have to tell you?"

"You can say what you like," said the fiki, "but I have told you the truth."

"I just wondered," said Mahmoud, "if he had paid you your reward?"

"I did not give him the body. That was to come later. Then there would be the reward."

"Not for the body," said Mahmoud. "For something else. Something that you had done for him."

"What had I done for him?" asked the fiki, and seemed genuinely bewildered.

"You tell me."

"How can I tell you," asked the fiki, "when I do not know?"

"Was that the first time you had met Narouz?"

"Yes."

"Are you sure? Are you sure that he had not already asked you to do something for him?"

"Such as?"

"Speak to the Man on his behalf?"

"We had not met before and he did not ask me to speak to the Man. I do not understand," said the fiki. "Why should I speak to the Man on his behalf?"

"To arrange a killing," said Mahmoud. "To arrange for a professional garotter to go on board the dahabeeyah that night and kill Leila Sekhmet."

The fiki drew in his breath sharply.

"Did you speak to the Man?" asked Mahmoud.

"No," said the fiki. "No."

Mahmoud got up from the desk, crossed the room to the window, pushed open the shutters and looked out. He stood there looking down into the courtyard as if he was searching for something, apparently having forgotten about the fiki entirely.

Owen took up the questioning.

"I believe you," he said. "I believe you did not talk to the Man."

"Well?" said the fiki uncertainly.

"I believe you killed the girl yourself."

"You have said I did not."

"That is my friend's story. It is not mine."

"Well?"

"You were seen with the body. How did that happen, I wonder?"

"You know already. I picked it up."

"How did you know it was there to pick up?"

"Someone told me."

"If that is true, give me his name."

The fiki was silent.

"There! You cannot. That is because there was no one."

The fiki deliberated on this for a while, then shrugged and looked at Owen.

"I shall have to take what comes," he said.

"Yes, you will. And I wonder if you know what is to come?"

"Prison," said the fiki confidently.

"Oh yes. But more. You see, you are about to be charged with being at least an accessory to murder. At least; for my story is that you were seen with the body and that you tried to hide it. These are not the actions of an innocent man. But even if they were, and what you say is true, that still makes you an accessory to murder."

"I played but a small part," said the fiki.

"You may think so but the law does not. And so," said Owen, "you will be punished not for a small part but as an equal in the whole."

"That cannot be so," said the fiki, disturbed.

"That is so. And furthermore," said Owen, "I have the power to make it so."

The fiki looked round the room as if in search of help. All he saw was Mahmoud's back.

"If there are no others," said Owen, "you will go to your fate alone."

"That is their good fortune," said the fiki heroically.

"It could be yours," said Owen, "if you wish."

The fiki looked at him with sudden interest.

"What do you mean, effendi?"

Owen noticed the "effendi" and smiled.

"You have a choice," he said. "It is this. You are going to be punished anyway. You will receive a long sentence for the arms smuggling. But eventually even a long sentence comes to an end."

He paused to let it sink in.

"Now here is the choice. Say nothing, and I swear to you that I shall charge you with being an accessory to murder

and will press for the maximum punishment. Say something—and it will depend on how much you say—and I may
let the other sentence suffice."

The fiki stood there for a long time.

"Who are you afraid of?" asked Owen.

"You know. He will have me killed."

"Not if he is himself dead. And that depends on what you
tell us. Not alone on that, for there are others. That may
help you to decide."

The fiki's head drooped. Once or twice he stirred and
seemed about to speak, but then his shoulders sagged again.

"Come," said Owen. "Who ordered the killing?"

The fiki tried to bring himself to speak. Owen waited.

"Come," he said again.

"The Man," whispered the fiki at last. "The Man."

"Good. And do you know the name of the man he sent?"

"Yes."

"That is good, too. We will come to that later. But first
there is a more important question. It is this. Who asked for
the girl to be killed?"

The fiki still hesitated.

"Someone approached you," said Owen, "and asked you
to speak to the Man and arrange for the girl to be killed.
Who was it?"

He waited.

"Was it Narouz?"

The fiki looked up, puzzled.

"No," he said. "It was not Narouz. Why—?"

"Who was it, then?"

"Hargazy," said the fiki.

⌒▨⌒

"I am very relieved," said Prince Narouz.

And took a drink.

"Very, very relieved."

He took another.

"To think that all this time this terrible man was plotting my ruin. No, worse than that: my death. I would have been killed, wouldn't I? I mean, if they had found me guilty of Leila's death."

"You have saving graces, Your Highness. You are an heir to the Khedive."

"I am not sure I like being an heir, if this is the kind of thing that happens to me."

They were sitting comfortably on divans in the Prince's *appartement*. In the street below Owen could hear men's voices.

"I shall, of course, be removing the guard."

The Prince held up a protesting hand.

"Not so fast, my dear fellow! There's no need to be in too much of a hurry. These are difficult times. Who knows what other desperate people may be about?"

"I think we have dealt with the threat now."

"You spoke of a gang, though, didn't you?" asked Narouz anxiously.

"Er, yes," said Owen. "I believe I did. Well, of course, I was referring loosely to his associates: the fiki, the Man, Abdul Mirzal—"

"Abdul Mirzal? Who is he?"

"He is the professional garotter. The fiki identified him to us."

"Behind bars, I trust?"

"Oh yes. Along with the rest of them. In fact, Prince, it has really been very satisfactory. Not only have we solved a crime which was preoccupying the Parquet and, of course, a potential embarrassment to you; we have rounded up a whole network of arms smugglers *and* at last managed to put the Man behind bars."

"Is behind bars enough?"

"It is only temporarily. Until the trial. Then, I think, he will be on his way to other things."

"I think," said Prince Narouz, "that until that actually happens we will retain the guard."

Owen bowed.

"As you wish, Your Highness."

At least there would be no complaint from Narouz about what had happened.

Narouz refilled his glass.

"What I cannot understand," he said, "is why that desperate fellow, Hargazy, should pick on me. I had never met him."

"You stood for something, Prince. You stood for everything he objected to. Power, privilege, rank, the old order. He wanted to sweep it all away."

"I'm all for reform myself," said Narouz, "but does one have to be quite so drastic?"

"I think he felt that it stood in the way of progress. There are," said Owen diplomatically, "surprisingly many people in Cairo who take that view."

"As a general point," said Narouz, "I suppose I can understand that. It is the particular application I object to. Why me?"

"I believe that was accident," said Owen, "the accident that you had become acquainted with Leila Sekhmet. It offered him, you see, an opportunity. He had made Miss Sekhmet's acquaintance some time previously but the relationship had lapsed. They met again, however, probably on the occasion of the first night of a friend's play—"

"Not that dreadful *New Roses in the Garden?*"

"Quite possibly. Anyway, at some point Miss Sekhmet told him about your invitation to her, to accompany you to Luxor on the dahabeeyah. That, I think, was when the idea came to him. Somewhat to her surprise, he encouraged her to go. After that, it was only a case of fixing the details, which he was able to do through the fiki."

Narouz shuddered.

"What a terrible man!"

"Yes. He saw Miss Sekhmet as something he could use. No more."

"Terrible!"

"I suppose it was easier to see her like that because she was a woman."

Narouz shook his head in commiseration.

"Our society is not altogether fortunate in the way it sees women," he said. "Now I myself value women highly."

ɷ

After the ceremony Paul took Owen back to the Consulate-General and gave him a drink in the garden.

"Congratulations!" he said, raising his glass.

"I feel a bit of a charlatan."

"Why?"

"Well, I mean—the Order of the Camel!"

"You saved his life, didn't you?"

"No."

"Well, he thinks you did, which comes to the same thing. Anyway, you've done other good things for the Khedive. You deserve the Camel."

They sat quietly for a moment among the roses and bougainvillea, enjoying the cool beauty of the Egyptian evening.

"The trouble is, though," said Paul, "that you solved it too late."

"Too late?"

"Yes. By the time you got him he had already built up a big head of steam in the radical press. The Khedive took cold feet and refused to sign."

"The Agreement's not been concluded, then?"

"No. It's all off."

Owen held up his glass against the sunset and studied the colors.

"So Hargazy got what he wanted after all," he said thoughtfully. "Or part of it."

He drained his glass and stood up.

"Club?" asked Paul.

"No. I'm off to see Zeinab."

"No," said Zeinab.

"What do you mean—'no'? I've done it, haven't I? I've found out who did it and put them in jail. What more do you want?"

"I want them dead."

"That will take ages. There's got to be the trial first."

"It won't do you any harm to wait. Men can't expect to have it all their own way."

Another thought struck him.

"What happens if some of the sentences are commuted? If they don't sentence them all to death?"

Zeinab just smiled.

To receive a free catalog of other Poisoned Pen Press titles, please contact us in one of the following ways:

Phone: 1-800-421-3976
Facsimile: 1-480-949-1707
Email: info@poisonedpenpress.com
Website: www.poisonedpenpress.com

Poisoned Pen Press
6962 E. First Ave. Ste 103
Scottsdale, AZ 85251

Printed in the United States
15716LVS00002B/315

9 781590 580530